"YOU KNOW, YOU HAVE A DECEITFUL STREAK IN YOU!"

"*My* intentions are good," Oregon said, so sincerely that Charity felt mollified. If he had stopped there, he would have been ahead, but he added, "Even if my actions aren't."

The teasing gleam was back in his eyes. She didn't know what she felt and she didn't have the smallest inkling about Oregon's feelings, so she kept quiet and didn't say a word.

"I've got to run," he said. The look in his green eyes was inviting, and she leaned toward him a fraction of an inch. His arms went around her instantly and he kissed her. Soundly. So soundly she forgot where she was, that she didn't want a casual affair. She wanted to wrap her arms around him and cling forever. . . .

SARA ORWIG

Oregon Brown

BANTAM BOOKS
NEW YORK · TORONTO · LONDON · SYDNEY · AUCKLAND

OREGON BROWN
A Bantam Fanfare Book / October 1993

Publishing History
Loveswept edition published August 1984

ISBN 0-553-56088-3

Published simultaneously in the United States and Canada

PRINTED IN THE UNITED STATES OF AMERICA
RAD   0 9 8 7 6 5 4 3 2 1

To Mary Grigg—and with thanks also to Grace Slaughter, George Dawes, and Tim Orwig

Oregon Brown

One

A bright full moon splashed an alabaster radiance over Enid, Oklahoma, and onto the shingled roof of a red brick, single-story house on Oak Street. Moonbeams skittered over immaculately landscaped beds of pink petunias, purple periwinkles, scarlet roses, and danced on the roof of the patio across the back of the house. Just beyond the shadowy patio, shades were drawn on a south bedroom window. Inside, the faint red glow from a radio dial added an orange tint to the old-fashioned maple furniture. In the hushed silence of midnight, a slumberous, baritone voice, husky and full-bodied, whispered, "Darlin', I've missed you. It's been so lonely . . ."

Charity Jane Webster stretched, her head rubbing the pillow, slender arms and legs brushing pale, cool sheets while the deep male voice sent a frothy tickle down her spine. She ran her fingers through the tangle of yellow curls that capped her head, a sigh of yearning escaping her full, curved lips. The radio dial's red glow kissed her wide cheekbones and her thick golden eyelashes.

"Darlin', here's one just for you, an oldie, 'Days of Wine and Roses.' "

She listened to the music, waiting for it to end to hear the velvety masculine voice that would strum over her quivering nerves. She was so lonesome. The late-night hours were the worst time of all. During the day she was busy, too busy to want someone, to really need someone else, but the long, empty nights were torment. She had found on station KKZF a late-night program of mood music called "Nighttime," with a disc jockey who had a golden voice, a rich, resonant baritone that floated into the bedroom, as tangible as a touch, nuzzling her senses, eliminating a fraction of her loneliness. Rory Craig Runyon. Each night she attempted to picture a face to go with that sexy, sensational voice.

He came on again, a lazy, raspy tiger's purr, rumbling up from his chest. "Darlin', did you like that? I hope so. It's one of my favorites. Now, darlin', it's your turn." He said the last in a breathy timbre that spooned hot liquid syrup down her spine and into her bloodstream. Each word in his special voice, like the notes of a cello, brushed a nebulous stroke over her flesh, a caress, making her tingle and ache, yet not feel so empty and alone. "It's your turn. . . ." The words, said in Rory Runyon's voice, held innuendo, implied intimacy.

"Darlin', let me know what you'd like to hear. Come on, give me a call. You know my number. It's eight four three . . ."

Charity blinked in the darkness. Each number

sank into her brain, keyed in permanently. Her hand drifted to the phone, then hesitated. Feeling ridiculous, she frowned at the radio dial. Should she call or not? The only answer was Rory Craig Runyon's thick, torrid voice pulsing slowly into her being. "Come on, darlin'. Let me know what you want to hear."

A phone buzzed on the program. Then Rory Runyon's marvelous voice whispered, "Hi, there." Pause. "Nancy, darlin', I thought you'd never call." Another pause. Charity wished she had called. "Sure. I'll play, 'You Don't Bring Me Flowers,' " he promised in a plaintive, hushed tone. "I'll play it, Nancy, just for you. Hang on there, darlin', and we'll listen together." Music came on and the voice went off.

Next time, she would call in. What harm would there be in a phone call? What harm would there be in calling a DJ and requesting a song? She looked at the door. She shouldn't be lonesome with her great-aunt down the hall, but Aunt Mattie was little company at night. Charity rubbed her forehead. What a muddle life could become! A year ago she had graduated from college with a degree in landscape architecture, had started her own small firm with money from her grandfather's brother, Uncle Hubert, and had been dating Ted Farnsworth. Now her business had failed, she had broken up with Ted months ago, and Uncle Hubert had died. With Uncle Hubert gone, Charity had only two relatives—Uncle Hubert's wife, Aunt Mattie, who was actually a great-aunt by marriage, and her mother's sister, Aunt Ziza. And whatever husband Ziza had at the moment. The mere thought of Ziza made Charity frown. She had lived with Ziza the first year after her parents' death, while Ziza divorced Roger, husband number five,

and married Wendell, husband number six. Charity
gave a small prayer of thanks she didn't have to take
care of Ziza. All she had to worry about were her
debts, her employment, and Aunt Mattie. Charity
moaned, but then her glum thoughts were interrupted by Rory Runyon. "Did you like that, Nancy?
Good. Call again, darlin'. 'Night."

" 'Night." It became two syllables in his soft mid-
western drawl. *'Nii-aight.* She envisioned sky-blue
eyes, curly black hair, a black-haired Tom Selleck.
Her sigh was audible.

"Here's another goodie for a balmy Sunday night.
Have you been outside tonight? It's great. Stars like
diamonds on black satin, spread across the heavens as
far as you can see. There's a little breeze running
across the prairie, racing over ripe wheat fields, just a
soft touch of warm May wind. A night for love, a
night to hold your hand . . . Let's add a little music
to the magic of the evening. Let a spring breeze
carry this song to your heart, darlin'. Straight from
me to you."

Charity blinked and swallowed hard. A song began playing, a haunting melody that relaxed Charity's tense muscles. The melodic voice singing the
ballad wasn't as enticing as the DJ who put on the
record. The voice sang, ". . . tied up in red ribbons
and blue paper . . ."

She blinked. Paper. She wished she hadn't heard
that word. The troubles of the day came rushing
back. She had inherited Uncle Hubert's house, the
care of Aunt Mattie, his newspaper, *The Enid Times,*
and a bushel of trouble. She didn't know anything
about running a paper. She could sell it. There was a
buyer. He lived right behind Uncle Hubert and Aunt
Mattie's. His yard backed up to theirs, but she

hadn't met him or looked over the high board fence that separated the two yards. Mr. O. O. Brown. It dawned on her suddenly that Mr. Brown was Rory Craig Runyon's boss. O. O. Brown owned the radio station and wanted to own the newspaper. But did she really want to sell? What would she do with the house and Aunt Mattie? What about her debts from her company?

She rolled onto her stomach to stare at the red glow from the radio. The music stopped. The inviting, lulling, sensuous voice came on again. "Now, darlin', it's your turn. Call me, I want to talk to you. Let me know what you like. Do you remember my number . . . ?"

How could she forget? She sat up, covers dropping around her hips as she dialed swiftly, hoping she would get the call through before the line was tied up.

The cottony words came through the telephone receiver into her ear, into her system. Something happened to Charity's heart. It stopped for a breathless minute. Dummy, she chided herself. But she couldn't speak, couldn't breathe. "Hi, Rory, this is . . ." She paused. Why hadn't her parents given her a sexy, contemporary woman's name? Something like Raquel or Brooke or Stephanie? She said, "This is Charity." It came out a squeak. She shook her head. What was the matter with her? Loneliness had unhinged her!

"Charity, darlin'."

Never, never in her life, not with Ted or anyone else, had her name been said in such a manner by such a voice. She melted into warm butter that could barely cling to the phone. She sank down in the bed feeling hot, idiotic, ten years younger than twenty-four, and she loved every second of it!

"Did you just catch the program or are you a regular?"

"I'm a regular. I love your program," she said softly, in a daze. A regular. All six nights since she had arrived in Enid.

He chuckled. Delicious tingles tickled nerves she didn't know existed. "That's good to hear. Thanks, darlin'. I feel better knowin' you're out there. What's your favorite tune, Charity?"

Just your voice, she thought. Wildly she racked her brain. Why hadn't she thought of a tune before she dialed? She couldn't think of any song except "The Star-Spangled Banner." "Oh, my favorite . . ." Help! Brain, think! " 'The Way We Were.' " She collapsed with relief.

" 'The Way We Were,' " he said, and she wished fervently it were true. "Hang on, darlin', while I put the music on." She would hang on forever. Where did she get this terrific loneliness? She hadn't even realized she was lonely until this last week. Maybe it was just leaving her friends and apartment in Tulsa, going to Enid, where she had lived with her great-aunt and uncle during three years of high school after her parents' death. The music began, and visions of Robert Redford danced into her mind. Maybe Rory Craig Runyon looked like the actor, thick blond hair, very clear blue eyes, flashing white teeth. That sexy, sensual voice could easily belong to someone who looked like Robert Redford.

And then he was back on the line, the music playing in the background.

"I'm not on the air now, darlin', the music is.

There's your song. For lonely moments, moments of love."

"Thanks, Rory."

"Don't hang up. I'm lonesome tonight, darlin'. We'll say a few words on the air after the song. I'll play 'The Way We Were' again tonight. Will you be listening later?"

"Yes." She would listen until dawn after this conversation.

"Good. I'm glad to know my audience. Charity's a beautiful name."

"It's a little old-fashioned." She didn't know what she was saying. Blue eyes danced in front of her. Blue eyes and bronzed, tanned skin. The man just had to have blue eyes. But, then again, they might be midnight-black, that lustrous darkness that was so mysterious, so . . . exciting.

"Rory . . ."

"Yes, darlin?"

There went her heart again. Oh, my! Enid was becoming more interesting. Maybe she wouldn't rush into selling the paper and returning to Tulsa. Into the phone she said, "What . . ." She hesitated, then reminded herself the call was anonymous. All he knew was her first name. She wouldn't meet him in person, so why worry about what he thought, or about being more forward than she had ever been in her life?

"What color eyes do you have?" She blushed furiously.

"My eyes? They're light-colored."

She knew it. Blue. "I thought so. And your hair's black," she murmured dreamily, visions dancing before her.

He chuckled. "You want my hair to be black? Let

me guess the color of yours. Charity. With a name like Charity . . ."

She held her breath, thankful he couldn't see her. Her mop of curls would hardly inspire a response. She looked like Miss Milkmaid of Smalltown, U.S.A.

"Charity—long, silky blond hair."

"How'd you guess!" she gasped, and her cheeks burned at the lie. Well, he was a fraction correct. It was blond.

"Ah, sweet Charity." She wriggled beneath the covers. How could a voice be so wonderful? So like a touch?

"Darlin', we're going back on the air."

He said it softly, almost apologetically. He added, "Call me again, will you?"

"Yes, Rory." In about two minutes.

"How'd you like that, Charity, darlin'?" she heard in her ear and over the radio.

"I loved it!" she said with absolute sincerity.

He chuckled. "I'm so glad! Keep in touch, darlin'. Thanks for calling me. 'Night."

" '*Nii-aight.*" She drew hers out just as much as he had. She didn't want to hang up the phone, to break the tenuous connection with Rory Craig Runyon. Blue eyes, black hair. Reluctantly she replaced the receiver and sank down, misty-eyed, melting beneath the covers to listen as he continued. "We're halfway into the first hour of a new day. But it's not day yet. It's still night, magic night, with stars and wind and dreams. Here's a song about the night. See if you like it."

Music wafted into the room, and Charity floated with it, carried by the sensuous voice of Rory Runyon. She replayed in her mind the way he had said her name. *Charity, darlin'.* Tingles coursed through her and she sighed. She touched her lips, then the small brown radio. " 'Night, Rory," she whispered, and closed her eyes to let Rory Craig Runyon's seductive voice lull her to sleep.

At about seven o'clock the next morning, Charity's eyes opened. She flung aside the covers, rose, stretched a body that was all rounded curves and softness, pale-skinned in the dusky room. When she raised the shades, she blinked as sunlight struck her eyes. Along with the sun she was hit in the face by the deluge of problems. Sorting through them, she decided to take one thing at a time, and the first thing was to continue helping Aunt Mattie dispense with Uncle Hubert's things.

She gazed at her plants filling the patio. They were the last remnants of her unsuccessful landscaping company. Pots of ferns, ivy, philodendrons, palms, the healthy, vigorous banana plant, airplane plants, a cactus, and dieffenbachia lined the patio across from the sturdy wooden porch swing. The swing was suspended from the ceiling and near the two old wooden rockers that had been used for years by her aunt and uncle.

Her gaze moved past the patio over the perfect yard. She knew where she had gotten her love of flowers and landscaping. It had come in the years since she had lived in this house, the short time that she had learned to grow flowers, when she'd watched Uncle Hubert putter with the beds, keeping the smallest offending weed out of the neat rows of flowers. Two cardinals dipped in the birdbath, their red wings fluttering, flinging crystal drops into the still morning air. At the back of the yard crepe myrtle blooms waved, glorious pink, purple, and fuchsia banners fluttering in an armada of green bushes. Flanking them was the high top of a weathered brown board fence separating the Webster yard from Mr. O. O. Brown's. Sycamore, mulberry, hackberry, and elm trees lined his side of the fence in a tangle of green limbs.

Knowing she'd have to start the day sometime, Charity quickly dressed in faded cut-offs, a yellow knit shirt, and sneakers, brushed her unruly mop of hair, and went down the hall to the kitchen to fix breakfast.

As she set the skillet on the stove, Aunt Mattie appeared. In a blue voile dress that clung to her thin shoulders, she looked as if she were headed for church. Trifocals slipping down her nose, she smiled at Charity.

" 'Morning, Charity."

" 'Morning, Aunt Mattie. How about scrambled eggs?"

"Won't your legs get cold, dear?" Her aunt took a loaf of bread out of the breadbox.

"No, I'm fine." Charity raised her voice. "Would you like scrambled eggs?"

"As soon as we eat, I want to work on the garage. For a man who loved neatness in his yard, Hubert had so much clutter in the house."

Charity shouted, "Do you have on your hearing aid?"

Her aunt smiled. "Yes, it's lovely out this morning."

Charity took a deep breath, shouting as loudly as possible. "Aunt Mattie! Where's your hearing aid?"

"What's that, dear?"

Charity pointed at her ear. "Hearing aid!"

"Oh, that dreadful thing. It makes me feel old, like a senior citizen. I don't want to wear it. Just raise your voice a little."

Frustrated, Charity cracked three eggs into a bowl and stirred vigorously. Even though Aunt Mattie was in her eighties, she didn't care to acknowledge that she might be beyond youth. Senior citizen. In her aunt's mind that classification must be reserved for those over one hundred.

Charity poured the eggs into the skillet, trying to push aside the problems, the worries about Aunt Mattie's care, as she cooked.

After breakfast she cleaned the kitchen, then joined Aunt Mattie to tackle the garage. As they went through boxes, she found two insurance policies that should have been filed for safekeeping. She carried them to her room to place them in the dresser drawer, hesitating as she gazed at herself in the mirror. She had put on a white cotton sailor's cap to keep the dust and cobwebs out of her curls. It made her look younger. She leaned forward to brush a smudge of dust off her cheek and saw something out of the corner of her eye. A slight movement. Her gaze shifted and froze. She looked into the reflection of two black eyes at the patio window.

Her heart stopped. In the sunny glare outside, through the blur of the screen, two black eyes had peered at her, then dropped down out of sight. A window-peeper? At ten o'clock in the morning? A prowler? She had caught the barest glimpse, but there had definitely been two dark eyes at the window. Her heart thudded, and she couldn't move. She thought of Aunt Mattie in the garage. She tiptoed across the room to a window. Holding her breath, she leaned forward cautiously and peered out onto the patio.

Two

The second shock was as jolting as the first. Relief changed to anger. To pure murderous rage. A long-faced white billy goat was eating her precious banana plant. Only two leaves were left!

"Ohhhh . . . get!" she screamed, flinging up the window. "Get!"

A short white tail wagged vigorously as the goat continued to chomp with zest.

"My baby! My banana plant!" she shrieked, looking at the devastation. The palm was now only a two-inch stub in a big pot, its remains scattered over the floor. A philodendron had vanished completely. A fern lay ravaged, its feathery stems tangled and trampled on the concrete. Even the cactus was gone!

With a cry of anger filling her throat, she dashed down the hall, through the kitchen, and out onto the patio, rushing at the offending animal.

"Get out!"

When she was two feet away, the goat turned. It had horns. It fastened its beady, black eyes on her, stomped its foot, switched its tail, and lowered its head. And charged, horns first. Two little horns that suddenly looked as if he had inherited them from a Texas Longhorn.

Charity's heart went into sudden shock again. She didn't think, she ran. She grabbed the screen door handle, but it slipped out of her hands.

Screaming in fright, she dashed for the porch swing, climbed up onto an arm, and clung to the chains as the goat rammed into the swing.

The swing sailed back, then forward, and hit him in the head. He gave an angry bleat, backed up, and shook his head.

"Get out of here!"

"Baaah!"

Rage burned in Charity. Pure white-hot rage, and chicken-yellow fear. "You cannibal!"

"Baaah!"

"Aunt Mattie! Help!"

Silence. The goat switched his tail, never taking his eyes from her. She knew it wouldn't do any good to call her aunt. The hearing aid was off and Aunt Mattie was seated in a rocker in front of the garage, where there was a breeze. She would rock and look at the old albums she'd found, albums of years past with Hubert, and would probably sit there for two more hours before she stirred.

"Goat, go home."

"Baaah."

Charity wondered where the goat could have come from. She looked around. The yard was fenced, the gates closed.

"You are a cannibal, a monster, a loathsome, mean, ornery, vicious, plant-eating animal."

"Baaah."

She shifted her weight, and the swing moved beneath her. She was hot, uncomfortable, angry, and afraid of the goat. Time crept past and her legs began to ache, the soles of her feet hurt where she perched on the arm of the swing, and her hands were cramped from gripping the chain. Cautiously she lowered one foot.

The goat's head lowered at the same time, his black eyes taking aim at the swing.

She raised her foot back to her perch. "Dammit."

"Baaah."

"You are a white-bellied, mangy, carnivorous, temerarious glutton!"

"Baaah."

"Baaah yourself, Billy Whiskers! You scrawny goat. You are wicked, you have no taste, no manners, no finesse, and no looks!"

"Baaah."

She shook her fist at him. "Go! Get your four skinny legs going back to wherever you came from. You murderer. You just killed . . . five plants! Five of my precious, healthy plants are in your fat bulging, rotten stomach!"

"Baaah."

She wiped the perspiration off her forehead, shifting her weight. He grunted, a little snort of breath, as if to remind her of his presence. She took off her sailor hat and threw it at him. It landed squarely on his head. He shook his head and the hat dropped at his feet. He bent down and began to nibble on it.

"No, dammit!"

If he heard, he ignored her.

"Goat, so help me, I'll get revenge. I'll have you put away. Leave my hat alone! It's not dessert!"

"Baaah."

She glared at him, and he returned to chewing a chunk out of the cotton brim.

"You damned billy goat." Or was it a nanny goat? Did nanny goats have horns! It had to be a male. Only a male would be that aggressive. Her legs did ache. While he chewed happily on the hat, she lowered her foot again. Carefully she lowered the other. The swing shook. The goat looked up, and then lowered his head.

She climbed back up on the arm. And stayed there for an eternity while robins and jays splashed in the bath, while bees hummed over the flowers and butterflies drifted across the yard. Shadows shortened and the sun climbed higher. Charity clung to the chain until the goat finally turned and trotted down the porch steps, across the yard, and disappeared behind the crepe myrtles.

And for the first time Charity noticed a plank missing in the board fence. The goat belonged to Mr. O. O. Brown! All her fury returned as she climbed down and eyed the devastation. Cautiously, she crossed the yard, keeping a wary eye out for the goat's return. Her heart thudded as she neared the fence. She didn't know if she could outrun the goat across the yard. The thought made her palms sweaty. Her anger was boiling like a seething volcano, ready to erupt molten rage all over Mr. O. O. Brown. She reached the fence, saw the board lying on the ground in Brown's yard, and realized there was nothing she could do about replacing it.

"Baaah."

Charity jumped violently. The goat was on the

other side of the fence, but not far away. She turned and ran for the house, her heart pounding. As she stepped into the kitchen, she gasped for breath, then gazed around the empty yard, at robins fluttering in the birdbath, butterflies still dipping over the periwinkles. But no pestiferous scraggly white face with two beady black eyes appeared.

She was quivering with rage. She stepped back onto the porch, scooped up her hat, and jammed it into her curls. Stalking through the house, she picked up a pen and paper and went out through the front door.

As she strode down the walk she glanced at her aunt, whose head was bent over an album. She'd only be gone a minute. If Mr. O. O. Brown was in his office, she would leave him a note.

Storming around the block, she headed toward the house that backed up to Aunt Mattie's. As she approached, she saw a white two-story house with large shade trees in the yard and no flower beds in sight, not even a shrub. She expected Mr. Brown to be at work, so another shock hit her when she saw a body filling a hammock tied between two shady sycamores. A very big body. Long enough to be over six feet tall. Shoulders broad enough to stretch the white net hammock. Her fury mounted at the sight. While he lay indolently in the shade, the idle rich with no worries or cares, his billy goat had demolished her plants and held her captive on the porch swing! She had a word or two for Mr. O. O. Brown!

She stomped up to the inert form and gazed down in silence for a few moments at muscular forearms sprinkled with red-gold hair; big, broad hands; a chest covered by a blue knit shirt that clung to muscles fit enough for a professional fighter; snug,

slim hips encased in faded, white-blue jeans; long
bare feet. The face and hair were hidden by a floppy,
broad-brimmed yellow straw hat.

The lazy, good-for-nothing bum. He might be
rich, since he owned the radio station and wanted to
buy the paper, but he was a bum nonetheless. And
definitely lazy. And he owned a lethal goat.

She tapped her feet, crossed her arms over her
breast, and cleared her throat.

Nothing. She cleared her throat again, louder this
time.

A slight, faint wheeze reached her ears.

"Damn you," she said.

A big freckled hand reach up slowly and gripped
the hat brim. The hat lowered. Thick, golden-red,
sun-kissed tangled curls appeared. Beneath them a
freckled forehead, then bushy red-gold, almost
brown, eyebrows. Then two green eyes, startlingly
green, with gold flecks in the center. A green that
was summer fields and emerald fire, that brushed the
heart with a promise of excitement. And eyes that
were as full of devilment as the old goat's had been.
Gleeful devilment that smiled and laughed and was
ready for fun, that coaxed the world to drop what it
was doing and come join the merriment.

She shot forth a glare, and it was deflected harm-
lessly off shatterproof green mirth.

The hat continued down over a crooked nose that
looked as if it had come into unfortunate contact
with a solid fist sometime in the past. The floppy
brim brushed broad freckled cheeks, drifting down
past his mouth.

A wide, well-shaped, slightly full mouth. An inviting mouth, with lips that looked . . . enticing, that

matched the green eyes perfectly, that looked as if they were meant to smile or kiss . . .

She forced her gaze to follow the hat brim down over a firm jaw. A very firm jaw. No doubt he was as stubborn as the goat he owned.

"Damn you," she said again, clearly.

He grinned, and it messed up her anger. The man did have a very alluring grin. A breathtaking grin. Dimples in both cheeks even! Gleaming white teeth. Oh, my. She said sternly, "Mr. Brown."

The grin widened. "At your service, honey. Did I do something wrong?"

Oh, dear. The enemy came well-armed. His voice was husky, golden and warm like the sun. Almost as nice as Rory Craig Runyon's. Almost, but not quite as deep and resonant.

"Do you own a goat?"

"Billy?" The grin got bigger. The green eyes danced wickedly, stirring her anger into a froth.

"That damned goat!" She yanked off her hat. "Look what he did!"

Mr. Brown studied her blond curls, his gaze lowering as leisurely as his hat had, drifting down to pause on her lips—a long pause that made her draw a deep breath—lowering over her knit shirt, pausing and getting a reaction she felt and hoped didn't show, down over her legs to her feet. The silky, husky voice said, "Honey, everything looks fine to me."

"Dammit, look at my hat!"

His gaze shifted. Placing his own hat on his chest, he reached up to take hers. His hand brushed her fingers. Warm flesh touching lightly, fleetingly, yet she noticed it just as much as if she had laid her hand on the hot sidewalk. Heat singed her skin, leaving a lingering reminder of his touch.

He turned the little white sailor cap in his big fingers, studying it carefully like a jeweler squinting at a diamond, before he rendered solemn judgment. "He really ruined a priceless object."

She looked at the hat, a familiar thing that she simply wore and washed and wore again and paid little heed to. Now she saw it as if for the first time. It was frayed from a multitude of washings, from bleach, from wear. Threads had popped and stuck little tendrils into the air.

She blushed with embarrassment and anger. "All right, it's no great prize. But he did ruin some things that were prizes. He ate my banana plant!"

"He did!"

Was the man laughing at her? Her fury was growing like a prickly cactus. He looked as if he were chewing the inside of his lip.

"Honey, I'm at a disadvantage. You know me, but I don't have the pleasure."

"I'm Charity Webster. Aunt Mattie lives behind you."

"I'll be damned!" he breathed softly, his dark brows drawing together momentarily while he soberly studied her. "Charity."

"Why do you own a goat?" She couldn't resist asking.

The grin returned, a teasing, mocking grin that fueled her anger. He settled back in the hammock, placing his hands behind his head and crossing his long legs as he gazed up at her. "I don't like yard work. I don't like to mow."

"What's that have to do with a goat?"

"He eats the grass."

Oh, lordy, the man was lazy! "Look, he ate my plants!"

"I'm sorry. I'll get you some more."

"They're big and expensive. He's a menace to the world. He's mean and ornery."

"Honey, don't let my goat get your goat."

The odious man thought the whole situation was funny! "Mr. Brown—"

"Hon, it's Oregon."

"What's Oregon?"

"My name. Oregon Oliver Brown. My mother was from Oregon."

He was as weird as he was aggravating. The goat belonged to him, all right. They suited each other perfectly! She drew herself up. "There's a board missing in your fence, and that goat can just come and go as he pleases."

"Don't blame him a bit. I may come over myself."

"Mr. B—"

"Oregon."

"Are you going to fix your fence?"

"Sure thing." He fanned himself with his hat.

"When?"

"Honey, you do get worked up about little things. Take life easy. I'm sorry about your uncle. I guess you've been here since the funeral."

"That's right. The flowers you sent were nice."

"Your aunt's a sweet little lady."

"That goat could do her in, you know."

"Billy wouldn't harm a flea."

"Oh, ho! Little do you know about your damned old goat!"

His eyes became thoughtful. "Did Billy hurt you?"

"No." She felt the fiery blush flood her cheeks, a telltale giveaway that something had happened between her and the goat. And Mr. Odious Oregon Oliver Brown wasn't going to let it pass unnoticed.

"He did do something to you!" He stopped fanning.

"That's not important. What's important are my plants."

"Hon, what did Billy do to you? He's so harmless. Did he bite you?" Again his gaze drifted slowly down over her thighs, her long bare legs, returning just as leisurely to her burning face. "You sure look all right."

"No, he didn't bite me! I'd just as soon not discuss my encounter with your goat. I want restitution and the fence fixed."

"I'll restitute whatever you want," he drawled in his sexy, husky voice, making it sound like the most suggestive thing she had heard in ages. And, aggravating her further, he added, "And I promise to fix the fence."

"When?"

"You do worry, don't you?" He was trampling her patience into the dust, mangling it as Billy had her plants.

"It's not a little thing! He could kill Aunt Mattie!"

"Billy?" Dark eyebrows shot up, and gleeful, wicked green devils capered wildly. "Now I have to know. What did Billy do to you?"

"If you must know—he chased me up onto the porch swing and kept me there for an hour!"

Oregon Brown sat up swiftly, plopping his bare feet on the ground, resting his elbows on his knees, bending his head down while he rubbed a broad hand across the back of his freckled neck below a thick brush of golden-red curls. And she knew he was hiding his laughter.

She was seething with rage. That damned goat had scared the wits out of her, kept her pinned on the swing for an hour, and his owner thought the whole episode was hilarious. She wanted to fling every one of her flowerpots at Oregon Brown.

"It's not funny, Mr. Brown."

He didn't answer, but the freckled hand on his neck rubbed faster. "I know," finally came out, muffled from his downturned head.

"Isn't it against the law to have a goat in town?"

"I have a permit."

"A goat permit?"

He raised his head. His lips were pressed tightly together, the corners of his mouth twitched, his cheeks were red, and his green eyes left no doubt whatsoever that Mr. Oregon Brown was about to split his sides with laughter.

He controlled it. The effort must have been stupendous. He flicked a glance at her and his lips tightened some more.

"How could you get a goat permit?"

"Because . . ." He paused and tried to keep his voice steady. "I'm not raising livestock. I have a live lawn mower."

She glanced at the bare yard. "It looks like a goat lives here," she said acidly, and his lips pursed, the dimples appearing in spite of his clamped jaw, and infuriating crinkles fanning out from his eyes. Laugh lines!

After a second he said, "Maybe I'd better come around and view the damage."

"That's fine, but first will you put the board in place on the fence so he can't come back?"

Oregon Brown stood up. Even barefoot he towered over her. She felt as if she were standing next to a Mack truck—except his lower half tapered down to such narrow hips. He had a massive chest and powerful arms that bulged with muscle. How had anyone who was so lazy developed such a set of muscles? It was like discovering that a sloth had the muscles of a tiger. The man must have moments when he moved. He took her arm. "Come on, honey. Let's get you acquainted with Billy."

She dug in her heels. "No! I don't want to see that goat again!"

"He's gentle as a lamb. Come on." Reluctantly she followed him around the house. There were tall shade trees and little else. The green grass was clipped close to the ground. There wasn't a stick of vegetation other than the short grass and tall trees and a wide elm stump by the gate. The yard looked neat, but not too appealing.

They reached the gate and he started to unfasten the black iron hinge.

"That goat doesn't like me."

"Billy loves you, I'm sure. How could he resist?"

Now, what did he mean by that remark? Her anger was swiftly transforming into fear. She did not care for Billy and she was sure the feeling was mutual. Very mutual.

Oregon Brown held the gate open, and when she brushed past him she caught a whiff of a clean male scent. But the enticing scent was forgotten when she entered the yard. Billy was chomping grass, his beady eyes focused on the ground. Oregon called, "Hey, Billy."

The goat raised its head, studied them a moment, and put its head down in its charging position.

"Oh, oh!" Charity started to back up. Suddenly the goat started running toward her, head down. Hard arms scooped her up against a chest shaking with laughter.

"We'd better get you out of here." Oregon stepped through the gate and kicked it shut, dropping the latch in place. "I'll be hornswoggled. He doesn't like you. Imagine that!" Oregon held her close, his wicked, merry eyes inches away, his full lips inches away. One of her arms was wound around his very warm, very solid neck, the other hand resting lightly against his broad chest.

She was trapped by his green-gold eyes, like green fields with golden sunlight sprinkled in them. Her heart began drumming with excitement.

"Billy just became a whole lot more valuable," Oregon said in a husky voice that drew attention from every nerve in her body.

"Now, look," she said, but her own voice was weak.

"I am looking, and I can't resist." He leaned forward the few inches necessary to brush her lips with his. It was the lightest breath of a touch, a whisper of warm flesh, of full, firm lips that barely touched, left, then returned swiftly to linger, to dally, to start a molten current flowing through her veins. His arms tightened, crushing her to his broad, warm chest. He smelled so good, so clean, like morning air after a rain. His lips were like velvet, as his tongue explored, touching hers, reveling in the moist warmth, tracing the inside of her lips to stir a response from her. For one full minute Charity Webster forgot everything in the whole world except strong arms, an enticing male scent, and sensuous, hot kisses.

Oregon walked a few steps and propped one bare foot on the tree stump, setting her on his thigh, which felt as firm beneath her rounded bottom as an iron bench. He wrapped both arms around her and crushed her softness to him, and then really kissed her. The dallying changed into a hot, thrusting demand, a searching that brought an instant response, that blanked out memory and logic from Charity's brain.

It was Charity's first kiss in too long, and it was as devastating as a tidal wave. Swamped and buffeted, she clung in a daze to Oregon Brown.

The world stopped turning, hung in the universe, wobbled crazily, went widdershins, then finally righted and settled in its normal course. Memory returned to Charity. Along with it came shock, then anger. She twisted violently, tearing her lips from his. "Put me down this instant. Dammit, I've had it with you, Oregon Brown! Don't kiss me." She wriggled off his leg and slipped to the ground, but his arms still held her waist and his propped-up leg pressed against her hip.

"You do swear a lot, Miss Charity Jane."

Another shock. "How did you know my name is Jane?"

Three

"And how'd you know it's 'Miss'?" she couldn't resist asking, and wished fervently that she didn't sound so breathless. And wished he would move his leg, his arms, just not stand so close.

"Your Aunt Mattie and Uncle Hubert have told me about you in great, glowing terms, about your business, your astute . . . mind, the cute little things you did in high school, how you lived with an Aunt Ziza before you came to stay with them, your breakup with Ted Farnsworth. I've listened to your letters . . ."

"Oh, no!" The day had started badly. With Oregon Brown's words it went downhill like an avalanche.

"Oh, yes. I know all about Theodore Farnsworth and . . . what was the name of the guy you dated three times after you broke up with Farnsworth? Brogan?"

"Dammit!" She gasped for breath. "That is none of your business any more than kissing me is!"

He grinned, that wide, infuriating grin that was as inviting as the yellow brick road. Well, she was immune to that grin. Absolutely. Inoculated by fury, rage, and anger.

He tilted her chin up. She tried to jerk away, but his fingers tightened on her jaw. "I kissed you because you needed to be kissed. I've heard the letters about how you're swearing off men, how terrible Farnsworth was, about how you decided to swear off men after Brogan . . ."

She managed to glare at him, but what was the matter with her heart, her lungs, her nerves? Her heart was thumping wildly, her lungs wouldn't function, and her nerves were overfunctioning because of a freckled-faced, tousled-headed, mulish man! "You keep out of my life!" she snapped.

"It's too interesting, hon," he said with maddening cheer. "You're very particular about men, you know that?"

"That's enough!"

He took hold of one of her hands before she could snatch it away. "Who's the current guy?"

"That's none of your business!" He was studying her hand as if he had never seen one in his life. One of his big fingers traced up and down her small, slender ones, trailing lightly between them, sending fiery tingles spreading upward that were more intense than such a light touch warranted. "I'll have to have a talk with Aunt Mattie about my letters," she added.

"Don't worry your sweet aunt." His eyes caught and held hers. "It's been fun to hear them. You have a nice sense of the ridiculous. Too much humor for

Mr. Farnsworth. That was good riddance. Brogan, too."

Odious Oregon Oliver Brown. He really was unbelievably odious. As irritating as his goat. "You and Billy belong together. What a perfect pair!"

He grinned and twisted a golden curl around his finger. "Such blond curls. Who has the curliest hair?"

"I don't really care!"

"Let's put our heads together and see." He leaned forward until his forehead touched hers and ran his big hand over the tops of their heads. Harmless, except his eyes were absorbing her and his lips were a fraction of an inch away. Too, too close. Then they weren't away at all. They brushed hers, melded with hers, and his bold tongue played havoc with her nerves.

This time she recovered faster, but the residual effect went deeper. Her mouth tingled and ached for more, but what did her lips know about anything?

He laughed and his dimples showed, twin indentations that were mirth and fun. The pesky man was "danger" in big red letters!

"I'll nail up the fence," he said, "then come over and look at the damage."

"You do that." His arms dropped away and she felt degrees cooler. She stomped off down the street, but from her head to her heels, the back of her tingled with an irresistible tug. She fought it past one more house, to the corner, then she had to yield. She looked back. He stood facing her, his muscled arms folded over his broad chest, grinning from freckled ear to freckled ear, sunshine creating a nimbus of red-gold curls around his head. He waved.

Charity gritted her teeth and marched around the corner. She hated the thought of selling Uncle

Hubert's paper to such a lazy, ornery man. A man who owned a goat so he wouldn't have to mow. Who lazed in a hammock at eleven in the morning. A man whose kiss was the devil's own temptation!

Now, why had she thought that? His kisses weren't temptation. No. She was just lonesome. They merely *seemed* better than Ted's or Hank Brogan's—Charity stopped in her tracks, then clamped her jaw shut until it ached. They merely *seemed* better because it had been so long since anyone had kissed her. It was loneliness. The same dreadful loneliness that made Rory Craig Runyon's voice sound so sexy, so tempting. She chewed on her lip. Mr. O. O. Brown was obnoxious! Probably the only reason the old goat didn't attack Brown was because the man was as big as a tank. The goat knew when he had met his match. Billy goat. What a name. No originality at all!

As she turned the next corner, she glanced overhead and saw gray clouds darkening the day, gathering, rolling swiftly across the sky while the wind blew in fierce gusts. They needed rain, but the clouds might blow right over without spilling a drop. Too bad a storm hadn't come early enough to keep Billy in his own backyard!

She marched up the walk; Aunt Mattie wasn't in sight. She found her aunt in the kitchen.

"Aunt Mattie," she shouted.

"Oh, dear, what's wrong?"

"Oh, you have on your hearing aid. Aunt Mattie, Mr. Brown will be over shortly. His goat got into our yard and ate up my plants this morning."

"Billy did?"

Charity felt a sinking feeling. "You know Billy?"

"That sweet little goat. Isn't he cute? Almost like a puppy."

Charity wanted to grind her teeth. "Aunt Mattie, that goat is mean as hel—as heck."

"Billy? He wouldn't harm a fly. You should've seen the way he let Hubert feed him little bites of cookies. Oregon took a board out of the fence so Billy could come over. Hubert would rock and Billy would stand on the patio, wagging his little tail, waiting for Hubert to break off a bite and hold it out. Then Billy would whisk it out of Hubert's hand so cutely." She sniffed and wiped her eyes while Charity wondered if O. O. Brown had two goats.

"It was Billy?"

"Yes. You'll love him."

"I don't believe so. Aunt Mattie, what does Mr. Brown do, besides owning the radio station?"

"He inherited his father's wheat land—there's oil on it. He has a man to manage the farm."

"I vaguely remember the Browns when I lived here during high school, but I don't remember Oregon Brown."

"Oh, no, dear. He's older than you. Oregon is thirty-two, and when you were in high school, he was already out of college. He'd moved to Virginia and was working on the *Washington Post*. He came back here after his parents' death. He's been here about six months now. He goes to the same church we do. You'll see him when we go."

Charity's mind was on something else. So he did know how to work. Journalism. No wonder he wanted the paper. "Aunt Mattie, please don't read my letters to Oregon Brown."

Aunt Mattie laughed. "Your letters are interesting,

and Oregon used to come sit on the patio with us and I'd read your latest letter."

The doorbell interrupted Charity's reply about the letters. "That's probably Mr. Brown," she said. For one fleeting moment she thought of his green eyes and wished she had brushed her hair and washed her face. Ridiculous. She compressed her lips and walked to the door and opened it.

The sight of Oregon Brown made her heart jump in the most absurd manner. She had been too long without kisses and hugs and dates, and her heart, her lips, her entire body didn't understand that she didn't want to notice the man standing before her. Down to her most insignificant little nerve, she noticed Oregon Brown. Noticed and quivered like willow branches in the summer wind. "You've already hammered that board in place?" she asked suspiciously.

"It fits on. I used to keep it off so Billy could come see your uncle Hubert. Wind blew it off last night." He leaned close to her throat and sniffed.

She looked down at his freckled cheek, the thick copper-colored lashes. His breath tickled her throat, and she had to fight an urge to jump back. "What are you doing?"

"I thought maybe it was your perfume that Billy didn't like. Mmmm, he couldn't dislike that fragrance. What is it?" He straightened.

Why did she suspect everything he said or did? Maybe it was the ever-present laughter in his eyes, as if he found her a constant source of amusement. She said, "It's Chloe. Billy just doesn't like me. He wasn't close enough to smell my perfume."

"Let's go look at the disaster area."

"Aunt Mattie!" she called as she led the way. "I

don't know where she is. She was just here." When
they reached the patio, Charity waved her arm in a
sweeping gesture. "There!"

He looked at the plants, the littered floor. His
gaze shifted to the porch swing, drifting up the chain
fastened to the ceiling, and his lips pursed again. His
brow furrowed, and her anger shot up accordingly.
"I'd like to see you hang up there an hour!" The
moment she said it she wished she could take it back.
Oregon Brown would never be treed by a goat. And
she knew it made his amusement deepen.

His eyes met hers. "I'll pay for everything." He
reached into a back pocket and withdrew a pencil
and notepad. "Let's sit down and you list them off."

She didn't want to sit down with Oregon Brown,
but she perched on the swing anyway. When he settled beside her, his broad shoulder touching hers
lightly, she had a ridiculous urge to jump up and
move. Determined not to be bothered by the man,
she studied her wrecked greenery instead of him. But
it was so difficult to ignore his fresh scent, the jean-
clad knee near hers, and his big hands moving close
to her.

She took a deep breath and said, "There's a philodendron, my banana plant, which was five—" Forgetting her resolve not to look at him, she turned
and glared accusingly at Oregon. The hint of longing
in his eyes startled her, and she instantly lost her train
of thought.

He waited for a moment, then his brows arched
questioningly. "Yes?"

He had the most enticing mouth, a beautifully
shaped upper lip and slightly full lower lip. He
smiled, and she realized he had asked her a question.

"You have a five-year-old banana plant?" he prompted.

"No, I don't know how old it was! What difference does its age make?"

Even though his expression remained impassive, she heard the suppressed laughter in his voice. "Charity, you said you had a banana plant that was five. I presumed you meant five years old."

She clenched her jaw. "It was five feet tall."

"Oh! Five feet tall. You didn't say that."

Damn the man. He was every bit as odious now as he had been earlier! She wished she knew how to stop a blush. His eyes were twinkling, but then the twinkle disappeared, replaced by a solemn look. Something was happening between them. He focused on her intently, sitting absolutely still. The air fairly crackled between them, and then it was gone. There was no air to breathe. She couldn't get the smallest breath. She couldn't talk. She couldn't pull her gaze away from Oregon Brown's. And he seemed to be suffering the same malady.

Only, he could move. He leaned over and kissed her. It was a light, questing kiss, his lips brushed hers, his knee barely pressed hers, and his hands didn't touch her. Again he brushed her lips with his, and it was so delectable! Her heart was thudding as his mouth settled on hers, parting her lips sweetly, and his tongue probed inside.

Somewhere in the depths of her being she felt the tension that gripped her tighten its hold. It became too constricting to bear. She struggled to gather her wits, vaguely aware that they weren't alone, that Mattie might appear any minute.

She straightened and leaned back. Oregon's mouth was parted from their kiss, and his lids were drooping over his blazing eyes. "Let's stick to the plants," she said, her voice a breathy whisper.

"Plants?"

She knew he was about to reach for her again. And she knew that part of her wanted him to, that she might not be able to resist. She stood up and crossed the patio to the plants. Her thumping heart didn't seem to realize she had moved away from the source of trouble. When she turned to look at Oregon, her pulse raced just as rapidly as before.

"He ate a five-foot banana plant." She could barely say the words. Oregon sat back, one foot on his knee, one arm stretched on the back of the swing. He was looking at her with such intensity she felt as if she were the first and only woman he had ever desired. With an effort she tore her gaze away. "You're not taking notes," she said.

"No, I forgot all about notes," he answered in a husky voice that was as sexy as his kiss.

"Well, write it down!" She risked looking at him.

One corner of his mouth lifted in a crooked grin that showed off his dimples and aggravated her. He looked so damned smug! As if he knew his kisses or his voice or his eyes could turn her knees to jelly. She raised her chin, and his grin widened.

"Will you stop that!" she snapped, then instantly wished she hadn't lost control. They were locked in a contest and he had just scored.

In a sensual, suggestive drawl that shook her to her toes, he asked, "Stop what?"

"Just write down the plants Billy ate." She ground out the words, hating the blush that burned her cheeks. She turned with determination to study another destroyed plant. "One palm, very healthy and very large."

"You like plants, don't you?"

"These were left from my landscaping business."

"Why did you have tropical plants in a landscape company?"

She tried to talk without looking at him, and it felt ridiculous. "People wanted me to do their patios, and occasionally I'd provide plants inside a house or business."

"You had a run of bad luck last summer. Hubert told me about the employee who lost control of the mower and drove through the plate-glass window and lobby of a building."

"Insurance covered most of that one, but they canceled the policy when another employee hit a parked car with a mower," she said to the stub of the palm. Her pulse was almost down to normal. She faced him. He smiled, and it wasn't as earthshaking as she had feared. It was pleasant, downright pleasant to look at Oregon Brown!

"Where'd you find the employees?"

She shrugged. "I had a hard time keeping any. They'd come and go. That was the biggest problem. Another one drove a mower into the lake in front of the Tower Center complex, and that really cost me. I had to pay for two more ride-on mowers and the damaged cars." She looked back at her plants. "Well, here's what's left of the fern. I guess it'll come out again and survive."

He made a note. "One fern."

"And he ate a cactus! How could he chew up a cactus?"

"Billy can crunch down most anything that doesn't get him first," Oregon said with an engaging grin. "What else?"

"As I said before, he ate my philodendron, but

don't worry about it. I can replace it easily." Suddenly she felt silly for making such an issue of five plants. To Oregon, who probably had seen whole wheat farms destroyed by hail, it must be absolutely absurd.

Oregon wrote it down anyway. "Anything else?"

"No, that's all. The plants were all I had left from my business, and somehow, as long as I had them, I felt as if I still had part of my business, as if I could start again." She shook her head. "I guess that sounds silly."

"Are you going to start over?"

"I'd like to, but I don't think I can for a long time." She didn't add the reason, but she had a suspicion Oregon Brown had already been informed about her debts to the last penny. She had written detailed letters to Uncle Hubert.

"Are you going to stay in Enid a while?"

"Yes. I have to decide what to do about Aunt Mattie. You know, now that I've calmed down, the whole thing doesn't seem that important. I don't need a five-foot banana plant or a palm tree. Maybe I wanted something that was mine to take care of. Just forget it, Oregon."

He rose, a coordinated unfolding of his big frame that made her feel as if the patio had suddenly shrunk and he was filling it completely. "It's nothing," he said easily. "Hereafter I'll keep Billy home. I can't imagine why he doesn't like you. Shows a definite lack of intelligence."

She smiled. "Thanks." Now, why couldn't Oregon be nice like that all the time? Just pleasant, instead of ornery and teasing and disturbing!

"I'll just go home this way. See you later."

He sauntered across the yard, and it was difficult

to stop watching him. She went to the kitchen, and when she looked out the window he had disappeared. Deciding that, for her own peace of mind, she should think about anything but him, she started cleaning the kitchen cabinets, changing shelf paper that hadn't been changed in years, and thought about Rory Runyon. An idea came to her and sent her into her room to make a list of song titles that she would request just to hear them repeated in Rory Runyon's husky voice.

That night, hours after Mattie had gone to bed, Charity bathed, pulled on a cotton nightie, and climbed into bed with the list of songs. At the same time that the familiar music started, a flash of lightning briefly illuminated the room. Outside a steady patter of raindrops was beating on the sloping patio roof. Charity settled against the pillows, closing her eyes to conjure up an image of Tom Selleck while she listened to the radio.

"Here we are again," Rory Runyon said. "It's 'Nighttime,' coming to you from Station KKZF with songs for midnight, soft, lulling music to put you in the mood. Have you been outside? There are rain clouds over us tonight, a gentle spring rain. Snuggle up, darlin'. We'll listen to music while raindrops pitter-pat on the windows."

Oh, how Charity wanted to snuggle up! His voice wrapped its shaggy warmth around her, enveloping her.

"Darlin' . . ." Pause. Charity opened her eyes and looked at the radio. Then, in a lazy baritone voice, so sexy she quivered from shoulder to knee, Rory continued. "This song is for you, darlin', just you." Didn't she wish! "Here's your song, darlin'. Here's 'Just You and Me.' "

She sank down, pulling the soft sheet to her chin while she listened to the music and wondered about Rory Runyon. Was he married? Did he have a woman in his life? Where did he live? She would ask Oregon Brown. Rory worked for Oregon, and surely Oregon would know whether the man was married or not. What a voice he had! "Just You and Me." Oh, to hear him say it again! Oregon had a sexy voice, too, but his personality ruined the effect. She did not want to think about Oregon Brown. She refused to think about him. Her lips tingled. She pressed them together, squeezed her eyes closed, and waited. The record finally finished.

" 'Just You and Me,' darlin'." Rory said. "There it is for you alone." His voice raised a fraction. "Here's something special—Captain Nemo's Fudge Bars. Fresh, delicious chocolate, melt-in-your mouth bites. I mean to tell you, these are mouth-waterin', oozy"—his voice lowered with every word, and every word wafted over Charity's simmering nerves, causing tremors—"sweet fudge, the thick, dark fudge like Momma used to make. Did you like to lick the pan?"

"Yes," Charity said, agonizing over his drawling pronunciation.

"Oh, so did I. Scrape a little bit of thick fuudge"—and "fudge" because a two-syllable, drawn-out word that made Charity take a long, deep breath—"off the pan and lick the last drop off the spoon. Well, I'll tell you what. If you like fudge, get some Captain Nemo Fudge Bars and unwrap the silver paper to bite off a chunk and *s-a-v-o-r* it"—Charity savored his voice, wriggling her hips unconsciously and running the tip of her tongue over her dry lips—"hold it in your mouth and just let it melt. That soft, creamy rich chocolate, so thick.

Let it melt. You'll agree Captain Nemo's Fudge Bars
are the most delicious candy you've ever tasted. Try
some soon, y'hear? Listen to that rain. Makes you
want to curl up where it's warm and dry, doesn't it?"
Charity wanted to curl up with Rory Runyon.

"Here's a song for a rainy night, for you, darlin',"
he said in a voice like a distant rumble of thunder.
"Here's 'I've Got Love on My Mind.' "

Charity wiggled her toes and wondered what
Rory was wearing, what kind of car he drove. Again
she went over his talk of the past few minutes, the
way he said certain words that made them sensuous,
suggestive, so sexy! At the same time she felt ridiculous. Never in her life had she acted so silly or felt so
lonesome. Maybe it was everything rolled together—
being away from home, away from her friends, the
worries, the loss of her business. Her attention returned to the radio as Rory came on to ask for requests. Charity reached for the phone and dialed,
only to receive a busy signal.

Aggravated, she listened to a young girl's giggly
voice talk to Rory Runyon.

"Rory, this is—" The girl giggled and finally
gasped, "Gloria!"

"Hi there, Gloria. Do you listen to 'Nighttime'
often?"

More giggles. Charity groaned. Gloria's squeaky
voice said, "I listen every night you're on."

"Do you, really? My goodness, what a fan you
are! What would you like to hear tonight?"

Charity rolled her eyes while she listened to giggles, but she did notice Rory's voice had raised from
the intimate, husky level and he wasn't using 'darlin'.
The man had some sense as well as a sexy voice. Glo-

ria giggled and gasped as she answered, "I'd like, 'Mean Mr. Mustard.' "

" 'Mean Mr. Mustard' it is!" Rory laughed softly. "Here he is, just for Gloria."

Disgusted, Charity threw back the covers and went to the kitchen to get a drink of water. As she stood at the kitchen sink, lightning flashed and she saw Oregon Brown's dark house. Oregon Brown. For an instant she remembered his kisses and felt as if an invisible bolt of lightning had streaked through the stormy sky and struck her. An electric jolt sizzled in her; then she shook her head to clear away the memory. The man could kiss. No doubt about it.

She hurried back to the bedroom and climbed into bed in time to hear the end of "Mean Mr. Mustard," and Gloria's final giggles. Then Rory's velvety voice glided like thick fog into the room.

Charity continued to listen and wasn't able to call in a request until the last half hour of the program. Finally she breathed ecstatically into the phone, "Rory, this is Charity."

"Charity, darlin'."

Oh, my! A dreamy sensation swirled in her "I thought you'd never call," he continued. "Just tune in, darlin'?"

"No. The line was busy before."

"You've listened since the beginning?" He sounded so satisfied! What difference would it make to him whether she listened or not?

"I've listened from the very first. Since you played 'Just You and Me.' "

"Good! What would you like to hear now?"

Ahhh. Even though she knew it from memory, she held the list beneath the red glow of the radio. It was a toss-up between "You Do Something to Me," and "You're My Thrill." She chose "You're My Thrill," and put heart and soul into it when she said it to him. "Rory, 'You're My Thrill.' " Her heart thudded violently, and she blushed.

" 'You're My Thrill,' darlin'," he repeated, only he changed the emphasis to "my." "Don't go 'way."

The music came on, an old instrumental song, then faded into the background as Rory said, "Darlin', I've been waiting for your call."

She was sure he said that to everyone. Everyone maybe except the gigglers and kids like Gloria. But she loved it anyway and sighed with satisfaction. "I've tried, Rory."

"I wish we were together. Listen to the rain, darlin'. I'd like to be beside you and we'd listen to the rain and I'd hold you." His voice dropped to a raspy purr. "Hold you and kiss you."

"Oh, you don't know me! You might feel differently if we met."

"We're going to have to meet soon, darlin'. Real soon."

"Rory, are you married?" The words came out as if of their own volition. Why had she asked him that? She sat up, burning with embarrassment.

"No, darlin', I'm not married. You're not either, are you?"

"No. I didn't mean to get so personal, but all I know is a voice. I get curious. . . ."

"Ask away, darlin'. I'll answer anything you want to know," he said in such intimate, suggestive tones that she blanked out completely. Not one question came to mind.

"No questions, darlin'?" He chuckled softly. She nestled in the soft, warm sheets and let his voice nuzzle her, sending her senses into a trembling longing that wiped out logical thought.

She listened in silence to the music, then Rory said, "Darlin', we're going back on the air and it's time to close. Call me tomorrow night, will you?"

"Oh, yes!"

"I'll think of you when I go home tonight. Sleep well, darlin'."

How could she sleep after that! She hung up the phone and listened to him say good night to her on the air, then play his last song and close. It was an hour before she drifted to sleep, and then she dreamed about green-gold eyes and aggravating dimples.

The next day, Tuesday, she woke to a sunny morning and dressed again in cut-offs and a blue T-shirt. Forgetting about Oregon and the plants, she helped Mattie clean out Uncle Hubert's desk and dresser, unaware of the change in the weather as the morning went on. Gray clouds appeared on the horizon and gradually moved overhead, bringing rumbles of thunder and the threat of more rain. About eleven o'clock the doorbell rang. Charity answered to find a uniformed man holding a large basket of philodendron. He peered at her over it. "Are you Miss Webster?"

"Yes," she answered. Beyond him she saw a truck with "Smith's Flowers" painted on the side.

"Well, I'm supposed to deliver some plants. Where do you want them?"

"Around the back, on the patio, please. I'll take this one."

"Sure." He handed over the basket and sauntered to the truck. Charity explained to Aunt Mattie and went out to the patio to tell the man where to set the plants. And discovered that Oregon had doubled the replacement. When the man had finished and left, Charity stood on the porch with two six-foot banana plants, two potted palms, two baskets of phil-odendron, one tall, spiky cactus and one short cactus, three kinds of ferns, two pots of ivy, a new airplane plant, and another dieffenbachia. As she surveyed the greenery, a mixture of emotions churned in her. She was embarrassed that she had demanded Oregon replace what Billy had destroyed, she was aggravated at his generosity, and she loved the plants. While she mulled it over, Aunt Mattie called to her, "Charity, here's Oregon."

With a startled glance at her cut-offs and T-shirt, she turned to the back door as it opened and he appeared. Her heart jumped ridiculously over the big smile he flashed at her. Dressed in a blue plaid cotton shirt and faded jeans, he was as forceful as ever. "I see the plants arrived," he said.

"Thanks, but you went beyond the call of duty. I feel silly for getting so angry about a bunch of plants."

He shrugged and strolled over to one of the banana plants, measuring its height against his shoulder. "That's okay. I owed them to you."

"Not twice as many! You sent me more than Billy ate."

He looked at her, and her body tingled from her head to her toes. "That's what I wanted to do."

End of subject. "Well, thank you. I love them!"

"Good." He walked back to her and braced one hand against the wall and leaned over her. "What else do you love besides plants, Charity Jane?"

"You ought to know, you've heard all the letters!" she snapped, losing the friendly warmth she had felt for about one minute toward Oregon. She wanted to run, but he had her blocked between the wall, the banana plants, his arm, and his body. Thunder rumbled and a flash of lightning crackled across the cloudy sky. To Charity's relief, the back door opened and Aunt Mattie appeared with a chilled pitcher of lemonade, ice cubes rattling and clinking as she struggled through the door. Oregon relieved her of the pitcher instantly, stretching his long arm over Charity's head to hold the door.

"It's almost lunchtime," Aunt Mattie said, "so I fixed some sandwiches."

Oregon grinned while Charity groaned inwardly. She didn't want to have lunch with him. A gust of wind whipped across the patio, bringing cooler air that smelled like rain.

"Oh, my." Aunt Mattie looked up. "Maybe we'll have to eat inside."

"I think so," Oregon squinted at the overcast sky. "Storm's coming up fast."

Another gust buffeted them, flinging gritty dust against Charity's bare legs. At the end of the patio, the dieffenbachia bent dangerously beneath the onslaught.

"Oh, the plants!" Charity cried. "You two go inside. I'll take in the ones that can't stand the wind."

While Oregon held the door for Aunt Mattie and disappeared behind her, Charity picked up a flowerpot and carried it to her room.

When she turned to leave the bedroom, she almost collided with Oregon and a large potted palm. He smiled through the fronds. "Thought I'd help."

"Thanks."

He was blocking her path, and slowly lowered the plant and looked around. "This is your bedroom."

A tingle, definitely unwanted, slipped down her

back. He had a sexy, vibrant voice. It didn't match the rest of him. In fairness, she realized that was a harsh judgment. If they had met under other circumstances, she might not have felt that way at all. His green eyes could be so inviting!

"Yes, it is," she said coolly. "Will you step aside, please? My plants will get ruined."

"Oh, sure. Just curious about where you sleep."

He could fill the most innocuous statement with such innuendo. She hurried outside, glad to be on the cool patio. Black clouds were boiling overhead, darkening the day to dusk. Wind gusts swept against the house, spattering big, cold drops of rain. She picked up another pot. Large hands took it from her. "I'll get these. Go inside; you'll get wet."

"I won't melt."

He grinned, and his gaze drifted down. "Guess you won't at that."

She clamped her jaw closed and grabbed another plant. He held the door while balancing a huge potted palm. They just set the plants down in the kitchen, but when Charity turned back to the porch, it was being drenched by the driving gray rain. Determined to save the remaining plants, she braved the cold water and snatched up two more pots.

One more trip outside and they were through. And soaked thoroughly. As they stood dripping on the kitchen floor, she looked at Oregon. He was staring at her, and his heated gaze slowly lowered over her face, her neck, her shoulders, then paused.

And she realized her wet shirt was plastered to her, molding the full, soft curves of her breasts and revealing her hardened nipples.

His eyes flicked up to hers, and he smiled lazily. She blushed furiously, certain he could feel the heat.

"I'll go change," she said.

"Here, Oregon." Aunt Mattie appeared from the hallway. "I brought you a towel. Give me your shirt and I'll put it in the dryer."

"Sure thing."

Charity fled the kitchen as if the demons of hell were after her. She didn't want to stand there and watch Oregon Brown take off his shirt. She hoped the mere thought didn't disable her heart.

She closed the bedroom door, but she couldn't shut out the feeling of invasion. Oregon Brown's aura lingered in the room, big and male and overwhelming.

She changed quickly into jeans, a white shirt, and sandals. She brushed her hair and applied a little blush, a dab of perfume. And braced herself for the next encounter as she stepped into the kitchen.

She didn't brace enough. Aunt Mattie and Oregon were sitting at the kitchen table, her aunt's back to the door and Oregon facing it. He had a small blue towel thrown carelessly across his shoulders with the ends draping over his chest, but it didn't hide his golden, freckled bare shoulders, the soft, curly red-gold fuzz that covered his impressive chest and tapered slightly to disappear beneath the low-slung damp jeans. When he saw her, he stood up in a sensuous movement that was filled with masculine grace.

He held out a chair while his languorous appraisal of her fouled up her brain. The room was suffocatingly hot; the walls were closing in. He was just so damned big and male and fit. There wasn't anywhere to look. She didn't want to meet his amused, knowing eyes. She didn't want to gaze at his powerful, sexy body—and it was so sexy! And she didn't want to ignore him, because it would reveal to him how disturbed she was. Another muddle brought on by Oregon Brown! She opted to look into his eyes and immediately wished she hadn't. He was very obviously amused.

The chair he had pulled out was next to his. Why hadn't he been so damned polite yesterday when he was stretched in his hammock? She didn't want to sit by him, but she wasn't going to let the man scare her. So she took the chair he offered.

As soon as she sat down, he shifted his chair away. The relief she felt was short-lived, because in two seconds she realized that he had moved so that he was in her view. He could look at her and it would be natural for her to look back at him. And if he stretched out his legs, they would touch hers.

"Now we can eat," Aunt Mattie said, oblivious of the broad bare chest that made Charity sure she couldn't swallow one bite. That towel was so tiny.

"Have a tuna sandwich, Charity. The wheat-bread sandwiches are tuna and the white-bread sandwiches are pimento cheese."

Charity reached for the plate. Just as her fingers closed on it, lightning crackled and an explosion reverberated in the storm. The kitchen lights blinked off.

four

Outside something crackled. Oregon rose and peered out the back door. He stepped outside, then returned swiftly. "Lightning hit the transformer. I'll call the fire department."

While Charity watched the blaze, the orange flames leaping up in spite of the rain, Oregon phoned the fire department, then tried in vain to get the electric company.

Within minutes the fire was over, but Oregon still couldn't get through to the electric company. He stood at the phone with his back to the room, and Charity stared without thinking at the splash of freckles over his golden shoulders, at his smooth, muscled back. He turned around, caught her staring, and grinned.

Blushing, she sat down at the table. "Don't you want to eat and call them later?"

He hung up the phone. "I think I'll do that."

Something thoughtful in his tone made her look sharply at him, but his expression was bland and he sat down. He accepted the plate of sandwiches, took one of each kind, then asked Aunt Mattie, "Do you have a freezer?"

"Just the refrigerator-freezer."

"Good. I think you're going to be without electricity for some time."

Charity had been about to take a bite from her sandwich, but she set it down. "Why do you think so?"

"Because I can't get the electric company. I've been through this before. It probably means the electricity is off other places in town. They repair in the order of the calls they get."

He took a bite of his sandwich. She had an uneasy feeling.

"If you'd like," he said to Aunt Mattie, "you can stay at my house until your electricity comes on."

Charity choked on a piece of tuna. She covered her mouth and tried to clear her throat. When she recovered, she asked, "What makes you think you have electricity? You're on the same block."

He looked too satisfied. "Same block, but a different transformer."

Aunt Mattie answered, serenely unaware of undercurrents, "Thank you, Oregon. You're a nice young man, but we'll stay here. We don't need lights."

Charity's mind was clipping along above the speed limit. Aunt Mattie went down with the sun. She didn't need electricity after dark, but no electricity—no radio! Charity would miss Rory Craig Runyon. And he was becoming important in her life. All day she wrestled with problems, every evening she fought loneliness. Rory Runyon was the bright moment in her life. She debated. As aggravating as Oregon Brown was, Rory Runyon was delightful.

"I won't be home tonight until very late," Oregon said casually.

The man had a date. That decided it. "Wait a minute, Aunt Mattie."

Green-gold eyes looked at her with an intensity that stopped breath, lungs, and heart. She blinked, gasped, and recovered enough to look outside at the sheets of rain striking the west kitchen windows. "I like to listen to the radio." She flicked a glance at Oregon.

A smile spread across his face, a satisfied, smug smile that almost made her refuse. Almost, but not quite. "We'll come if we don't have electricity. And if the rain lets up enough to get Aunt Mattie over."

"It will," he said with no room for doubt.

She had a feeling he was right. Aunt Mattie took a sip of hot coffee, then said, "That's so nice. Charity doesn't go to bed as early as I do."

Charity sent up a silent plea. Aunt Mattie, don't talk about my going to bed. The powers that be didn't acknowledge the prayer. "She's a night owl," Aunt Mattie continued. "And up out of bed early in the morning. Just not enough sleep for a healthy young woman."

Oregon looked at her, his eyes dancing with devilment. "Bed uncomfortable? Are you too tense to sleep?"

She blushed. He knew exactly what he was doing. "No. Will this rain be good for your wheat or have we had too much lately?"

He grinned an infuriating grin. "We haven't had enough rain. It'll be good for the wheat. Should be good for sleeping too. It'll be cool. I always like to sleep in the . . ." Charity held her breath with his pause, letting it out when he said, ". . . rain."

"Oh, my, yes," Aunt Mattie said. "I'll have to get out the blankets tonight."

"No, you won't, Mattie. You'll be at my house"— Oregon looked at Charity—"in my beds. I'll get out the blankets. Maybe you just need change, Charity. Maybe in my bed you won't have insomnia."

Charity fumed, looking down at her sandwich. Odious Oregon Brown fit. She wanted to tell him they wouldn't come, but she wasn't about to give up hearing Rory Runyon. Thank goodness Oregon would be out! Momentarily she wondered who dated him. What kind of woman would put up with him? Maybe he won her over with his spectacular kisses—

Someone might just as well have dumped ice water on her. Startled, she looked up to find him watching her curiously. She dropped her gaze, feeling confused. Why had she thought his kisses were spectacular?

"Charity." Aunt Mattie's voice sounded persistent.

"Yes?"

"Oregon asked if you like eggs or pancakes better?"

"Sorry, I didn't hear you." She hated his pesky smile. "Eggs. Pancakes are fattening."

His green eyes assessed her. "That shouldn't worry you, Charity."

"Thank you."

He grinned.

They ate in silence for a few minutes, then Aunt Mattie said, "Charity, we got a letter from Ziza this morning." She glanced at Oregon. "I've told you about Ziza"—Charity wondered if there was anything Mattie hadn't told Oregon—"Charity's aunt on her mother's side of the family." Aunt Mattie turned back to Charity. "She sent an announcement of her wedding."

"Again! That's number eight! I didn't know she was going with anyone."

"She said it was a whirlwind romance and they married three weeks ago in Mexico City. He's an insurance salesman and they'll live in Kansas City. They're coming to see us this weekend."

"To Enid?" Charity had a sinking feeling. She had enough problems without Ziza's adding to them. Chaos seemed to follow her tall, dark-haired aunt. She glanced at Oregon and detected a thoughtful expression in his eyes.

"Her brother-in-law, Rolf, lives in Oklahoma City, so they'll meet here. Rolf's single and she wants you to meet him."

"Oh, lordy," Charity groaned, and blushed. Why, oh, why did Aunt Mattie bring it up in front of Oregon? She refused to look at him and searched desperately in her mind for another topic. Her desperation mushroomed as Aunt Mattie turned to Oregon and added, "It worries Ziza that Charity isn't married."

"You don't say."

Charity glanced at him sharply and immediately regretted it. He grinned at her and asked with great innocence, "You anxious to get married, Charity?"

"No. The idea of spending the rest of my life with some of the men I've met is too awful for words!"

His eyes had a wickedly gleeful expression. "Too awful! Do tell. What would you like in a husband?"

Would this conversation never end? She wanted to gnash her teeth and tell Oregon to go to hell.

"Kindness. I'd definitely want kindness. I think I'll have some more lemonade." Her glass was three-fourths full. She rose to get the pitcher and returned to the table. "Would you care for more, Aunt Mattie?"

Aunt Mattie shook her head.

"Kindness," Oregon mused. "Well, kindness is an admirable quality."

"What's Ziza's husband's name?" Charity asked Aunt Mattie, fighting the desire to pour the lemonade on Oregon's head.

"It's Bernard Feathers," Aunt Mattie said.

"Ziza Feathers. Will they be here long?"

"She didn't say. You know Ziza."

Too well, Charity knew Ziza. She glanced at Oregon reluctantly. "Do you care for more lemonade?"

"Yes, please. So you want a kind husband. What else?"

"A silent one."

He grinned, the dimples appeared, and she almost poured the lemonade right into his lap. If she did, it would be her luck that he would stay at their house until his jeans dried. "Kind and silent," he said. "Might be a little dull, Charity."

She compressed her lips and set the pitcher on the counter, her back to Oregon while she tried to control her temper. With an effort she smiled at him as she sat down. "I prefer everything quiet and peaceful. Very quiet."

Aunt Mattie laughed and said, "Oh, Charity, that's a good one! It's always fun when you're here." She sobered and peered through her trifocals. "I don't know what I'll do when you go." Her eyes filled with tears suddenly, and Charity reached across the table to squeeze her aunt's cold fingers.

"I'm here and I'm not leaving any time soon. Now, don't you worry." Aunt Mattie smiled and Charity turned to glare at Oregon, as if to lay the blame square at his feet for disturbing her aunt, but she clashed with a probing, solemn look that made her lower her lashes swiftly.

Even though the conversation turned to a safe topic, Charity thought the lunch would never end, the rain wouldn't let up, and Oregon wouldn't ever leave, but he did. After he pulled on his dry shirt, leaving it open, he handed the towel to Charity. It was warm from his body heat. She dropped in onto a chair as if it were on fire and followed him to the kitchen door. "I'll go through the back," he said.

They stood on the patio a moment. Water dripped off the roof and trees, an orchestra of plops splashing on the concrete, into puddles, and on the grass. Across the western sky a rainbow arced bright colors against an expanse of gray-blue. Charity found the golden furred chest beside her more intriguing than the sweeping colors in the sky, though.

"See you tonight," he said. "Call me and I'll come get you so your aunt won't get wet."

"Thanks, I can drive."

'Okay." He strode across the wet grass, sprang easily to the top of the fence, then dropped out of sight on the other side.

Charity spent the rest of the day alternately puttering in the garage, cleaning and sorting through things, and calling the electric company. When she finally connected, a man said lightning had knocked out lines all over Enid and it might be twenty-four hours before they could get to her neighborhood.

Disgruntled, she replaced the receiver. That meant a night at Oregon Brown's. He would be away, so it shouldn't be too disastrous. She returned to cleaning and tried not to think about the coming night.

Later she and Aunt Mattie ate another cold meal, then Charity bathed, packed a few things, gathered them up along with Aunt Mattie's, and drove around the block to Oregon Brown's.

He greeted them at the door. Tight wheat-colored jeans molded his legs, and a cream-colored knit shirt covered his chest, its color flattering to his ruddy complexion and golden hair. His tan leather boots made him tower over her more than ever. He looked appealing, very much so. If she hadn't known about his personality, she would have been quite impressed. Her heart was impressed anyway and beat double time when she passed him to enter the house.

It was a surprisingly nice house. She had expected clutter and something goatlike. Instead there were high ceilings and dark mahogany woodwork, deep beige carpeting, and comfortable, obviously expensive cherry-wood furniture.

"I'll show you your bedrooms," Oregon said cheerfully. He tucked the two small suitcases under one arm and took Aunt Mattie's arm with his other hand, leaving Charity to trail behind.

"Mattie, I gave you the downstairs bedroom, my room, so you won't have to climb the stairs."

Charity almost missed her step. She glared at Oregon's thick red-gold curls. So he would sleep upstairs with her! Getting to hear Rory Runyon was going to cost her some peace of mind.

"Would you like something to eat?" Oregon asked.

Aunt Mattie laughed. "Oh, dear me, no! We just ate. And it's my bedtime. Just let me put these old bones down to rest."

"Sure. Here we are." He led Aunt Mattie into a room while Charity stood in the doorway. It was his room, all right. Aunt Mattie would get lost in the king-sized bed that was covered by a quilted emerald-colored spread. Two brown leather wing chairs were in front of a stone fireplace. A large brown desk held neat stacks of papers and a telephone. A television was in one corner, plants lined the windows, bookshelves covered one wall.

With a vague, uneasy feeling, Charity wondered if they had prevented Oregon from bringing his date home tonight. That was neither here nor there; she shrugged the thought away. Oregon took her arm. "Mattie, Charity will come down and help you in a minute. Let me show her where she'll sleep before I go."

"Run along, dears. I can manage."

Dears. Charity was acutely aware of his fingers fastened lightly around her upper arm. They left Aunt Mattie, and Charity felt as if she had been flung to the lions. A fresh, male scent invaded her senses with subtle insistence, an odor of summer clover, of the outdoors. As they climbed the steps side by side, she longed to tell him to remove his fingers from her arm, but she didn't want to make an issue of it.

"Today," she said, "our attorney talked about your offer for Uncle Hubert's newspaper." She slanted a look at him. "You haven't mentioned it."

"I'm interested. There's no hurry and I didn't want to rush you or Mattie. I told Jack to wait until next week to call."

She mulled over his answer. It seemed typical of his laid-back style, and she was relieved that he wouldn't pressure her for an answer. They had reached the upper hallway, which had four doors opening off it. He led the way to the farthest door on the right. She hoped his would be the farthest door on the left.

"Here we are." He opened the door and waited. To her relief his fingers dropped away from her arm. She entered a spacious bedroom with antique mahogany furniture, a large mirrored armoire, an ornately carved dresser, and a four-poster bed. It was neat and would have been a pleasant, comfortable guest bedroom except for one thing. The bed had a flaming scarlet spread turned down over black satin sheets. Black as midnight! "Maybe Aunt Mattie should stay here," she said dryly.

"This is definitely you."

Her cheeks grew warm. "I'm not the black-satin-sheet type."

"Try them and see," he said lightly as he set her suitcase down. "There's a clock-radio by the bed. Want me to show you how to set it?"

"I brought my own."

"Like to listen to the radio?"

"Yes, but I'll keep it low. It won't disturb you."

"Oh, don't worry about that. Listen all you want. What kind of music do you like?"

She didn't like his persistent questions, but she remembered Oregon was Rory's boss. She would put in a plug for Rory.

"My favorite program is one on your station."

"Do tell!"

His green eyes were beginning to look mischievous again. Well, give Rory a compliment and drop it. No doubt Oregon took credit for everything that came from his station. "Yes. I like 'Nighttime,' with Rory Runyon."

"Ahhh, you like Runyon's style."

"Yes." So there, Mr. Oregon Brown! Take a lesson.

His eyes narrowed. "You like the music or Rory Runyon?" he asked in a matter-of-fact voice, as if he were conducting a poll. No harm in telling him.

"I like Rory Runyon." She waited two heartbeats to see if he would try to make something of that. When he didn't she warmed to her subject. "He's a marvelous DJ."

"Thank you. Why do you think so?"

"Hmmm. His voice, his manner . . ." She paused again, but Oregon merely gazed back blandly. "He's so . . . so . . ."

"Sexy?" he suggested softly.

She blushed and snapped her mouth shut. She should have known better!

"There's nothing wrong with sexy," he said. "Why the blush, Charity?" His finger sailed over her cheek, leaving a trail of silvery tingles fluttering in its wake.

"Sex is personal," she muttered angrily. "I don't care to discuss sex with you."

"I can't think of a more interesting subject to discuss with you."

She shot him a dark look and saw the laughter in his eyes. "You can be so damned aggravating. I feel like packing and going home!"

He waved his arm at the door. "I'm not holding you here."

She glared at him. Once more she had to choose between Rory Runyon and Oregon Brown. Put up with one to have the other.

"You won't get to hear Rory Runyon if you go," he said.

"I'll stay. In spite of circumstances," she said with

as much ice as possible. It was difficult to project ice when you were five three, had delinquent blond curls that would never behave, and big blue eyes that belonged on a doll, but she gave it a try. And while she was busy trying to be icy, Oregon moved closer.

"You know, Charity," he said, his voice thoughtful, "you really do need to be kissed."

"I—"

Someday she would learn. Too late now, for his mouth was over her open one. His long arms, steel bands, fitted her to his broad chest, against a heart that thudded while his tongue took control and ended her arguments, stirred a response, and took her breath away. Completely. And she was most thoroughly kissed.

Her system couldn't get the message that she was aggravated with Oregon Brown, that heart and pulse and metabolism should not respond. They responded shamelessly, instantly, and totally. Her arms wound around his neck and clung. He felt so good!

His big hand drifted slowly, devastatingly, down her spine, then he pressed her soft, rounded bottom to him. His hand lingered, then changed course, moving upward, molding her curves, brushing the underside of her breast. She moaned, but the sound was muffled by Oregon's mouth.

His hard arms encircled her and he picked her up. He carried her to the bed and gently lowered her to it, then lay down beside her and pulled her into his arms. A degree of sanity returned to Charity and she pushed.

He stopped instantly. She looked up at him, into green eyes darkened by passion, eyes that were like emerald seas that coaxed her to set sail, to drift in their green-gold currents. She rolled away. "Will you stop?"

"I did a second ago." He shifted onto his back and put his hands behind his head.

"I thought you were going out."

"I am, in a minute."

His words, in his husky, sexy timbre, tripped her heart into flight. He lay so close, his big body so aroused. Charity swallowed and was surprised that her throat hurt, that her whole body ached.

He smiled and stood up, and she turned her back to him.

"What's the matter, Charity?"

"Nothing."

A kiss brushed the nape of her neck, his husky voice coming with his minty breath. "See you later."

And then he was gone. Warmth, disturbing and erotic, went with him. Relief came, and, to her surprise, disappointment. She wished he hadn't been going out. The thought shocked her. Long ago she had vowed she would never be trapped into the situation her Aunt Ziza was in—drifting from husband to husband or relationship to relationship because of loneliness or vulnerability. After having lived through one of Aunt Ziza's divorces and marriages, Charity had vowed she would never enter into a relationship lightly. If she were to commit herself seriously to a man, she wanted to know him long and well first. Oregon Brown was a definite threat to her resolution! Thoughts of Oregon sent her to her suitcase for the list of four songs she wanted to request, just to hear Rory Runyon say the words back to her again like the night before.

"I'll Have to Say I Love You in a Song," "You Are So Beautiful"—She blushed just looking at that one. No one had ever said that to her. This was her only chance—"When a Man Loves a Woman" and "Touch Me in the Morning."

She moved the last one up on the list. She just had to hear him say, "Touch me . . ."

She laid aside the list and went downstairs to see about Aunt Mattie. She was already asleep, so Charity turned out the light and closed the door, then decided to prowl through Oregon's house. The decor was amazingly lovely. There were antique cut-glass crystal pitchers and bowls filling an old-fashioned curved glass front china cabinet. The kitchen was filled with modern appliances, warm oak cabinets, and had a bright yellow floor. Oregon obviously loved color. The house was a rainbow of tasteful colors set against a pale beige carpet. The living room had a big fireplace, a Chickering grand piano, a stereo console, and comfortable furniture.

It didn't fit him. In her mind he belonged in a grass shack on a tropical island. He and Billy. She gazed out one of the kitchen windows, shivering. Thank goodness the goat wasn't a house pet!

Finally it was time for 'Nighttime' and Rory Runyon's adorable, husky voice. She put on a red-and-white polka-dot nightie, picked up her list, placed the phone beside the bed, and turned on the radio.

The black satin sheets were cool against her skin. She ran her fingers across a pillow slip. Why did Oregon have black satin sheets? She didn't want to speculate on that one! But for a fleeting moment she remembered lying in his arms. It had felt good. She closed her eyes and thought about Oregon's embrace, his kiss, and Rory Runyon.

She made a mental note to brave the teasing and

ask Oregon for a picture of Rory Runyon. Then Rory's husky voice glided into the room, circling, floating to caress her waiting nerves, to take her breath away.

"Hi, darlin', I couldn't wait to be with you. We're going to listen to some music. Just you and me, darlin'. Let's do this together."

A song began and Charity gulped and blinked in the darkness, remembering Oregon's hot kiss. Her body was aching. She wanted to be kissed, to be touched. She rolled over and peered at the radio. A brown radio. She tried to envision Tom Selleck with black hair, but all she could see were green-gold eyes and freckles.

She sat up. Oregon Brown was interfering with Rory Runyon. The damned green eyes and curly golden-red hair and freckles interfered, along with broad shoulders and muscles and deviltry!

She gritted her teeth and wriggled her hips in a determined effort to get Oregon Brown firmly out of her mind. If only she could think about Oregon's kiss and see Rory's face, just fantasize and have the perfect—She blinked. The perfect male? Oregon's kisses were that good?

The record ended and Rory came on, his voice taking away her bad images, her worrisome thoughts. She sank down in bed, soothed by velvety, smooth tones that caressed her in the dark. And he finally came to what she had been waiting for. His voice drifted over her senses as he said, "Darlin', call me."

She did with such haste, she almost dropped the phone. Then his voice reached her through the line.

"Rory, this is Charity."

"Charity, darlin'." She melted. "I've been waitin'

for you to call me," he whispered. "I was afraid you wouldn't. What song would you like to hear, darlin'?"

She swallowed. Her palms were damp and a blush scorched her cheeks. Thank goodness for darkness, for anonymity!

"Will you play 'I'll Have to Say I Love You in a Song'?"

"Darlin', of course. I'd like to hold you in my arms, Charity, while I play this."

Charity thought she would faint. His marvelous voice, the seductive words, made her ache as her hips moved slightly. His voice didn't ease her longing; it stirred it to monumental proportions.

She closed her eyes and clutched the phone while hot, golden words flowed over her, burning as they went down, starting a fire in her lower regions.

"Would you like to be in my arms, darlin'?"

"Yes . . ." Lord, yes!

"I want to hold you next to my heart. Settle your head back into my shoulder. Here, darlin'. Here's 'I'll Have to Say . . . I Love You . . . in a Song.' "

The pauses almost finished her off. "I Love You," said in his fluid, amber voice, made her groan in the darkness.

"Charity . . ."

"Yes, Rory?" She waited breathlessly.

"I'm glad you called. I really have been waiting."

He sounded as if he meant it. She wondered how many women he told that to, but didn't really care. It sounded so good!

"My blond Charity. I'd like to hold you for this song. Can you imagine my arms around you?"

She couldn't answer. She tried to breathe and finally whispered, "Yes." She remembered strong arms, a warm, male body, and tried to forget the face that went with it.

"Can you imagine my lips on yours?"

Shocked at his boldness, she looked at the phone. Lord, the man was coming on strong! Since when did disc jockeys get so personal? "Is this going to be an obscene phone call? You're sure we're not on the air?"

He chuckled and she wilted. Each little baritone sound carried a seductive tickle. "We're not on the air, darlin'. The 'I Love You' song is."

Her heart might not survive the song.

"Charity, can you imagine my kiss? I'd like to kiss you, darlin'."

Her eyes widened and she stared at the receiver again. He might get himself in trouble if he said that to every woman who called KKZF. "Do you say that to everyone?"

"This is a first."

A first! Something soft wrapped around her heart and squeezed lightly.

"Charity, I mean it. I'd like to kiss you, darlin'."

"I'd like you to." Dreamily, she added, "And that's a first."

"First time you've wanted—"

"First time I've told a man I wanted his kiss," she interrupted him hastily.

"We'll have a lot of firsts, Charity. I'd like to touch your soft cheeks, your silky hair, to hold you, to talk to you, to kiss you and caress you. . . ."

Charity shifted in bed, squeezed her eyes shut, moistened her lips unconsciously. This radio business wasn't good for her constitution. Rory Craig Runyon's voice was a health hazard. She wanted to ask him why he had singled her out so swiftly from his other callers, but she was afraid. And she didn't really believe that she was the only one.

"Charity, the song's going to end. Will you call me back tonight?"

"Yes," she whispered.

"You have another song to request?"

"As a matter of fact, I do."

"Good, darlin'. That's my girl. Here we go on the air."

The music ended and he asked, "How's that, darlin'? Did you like your song?"

"I loved it," she gasped.

" 'I'll Have to Say I Love You in a Song.' What a nice way to say it. This is a good night for a song like that. It's nice outside, a beautiful May evening, about sixty-five degrees, stars out, not a cloud in sight. Wasn't that a storm we had today? Now the clouds are gone and it's a perfect night to hold you close and listen to music. Call me again, Charity. 'Nii-aight, darlin'."

" 'Night, Rory." Charity collapsed on the pillow, clinging to the phone. She longed to be held. She ground her teeth and groaned. A big golden body was damned difficult to forget.

She spent the next two hours, all of Rory Runyon's 'Nighttime,' alternately agonizing and delighting in his voice. She called twice more. The second time she lost her courage and couldn't ask for "You Are So Beautiful." It might be too obvious. Rory Runyon was sexy, and he might also be smart. So she requested "When a Man Loves a Woman."

" 'When a Man Loves a Woman,' " he repeated, after putting on the record and telling her their conversation wasn't on the air. "Charity, want to know how I'd love a woman?"

The man was oversexed. "Yes," she whispered, trembling, blushing in the dark bedroom. She wanted to hear, but she didn't want to. She hoped he wouldn't get obscene. She couldn't hang up on Rory Runyon. She held her breath as he whispered throatily, his voice coming up as if from the molten center of the earth, slowly rising to air, "I'd hold you next to my heart, Charity."

She let out her breath. Nothing scandalous so far. Just delightful, so sexy! "I'd kiss you all night long, kiss you so slowly, darlin'. Charity, are you there?"

It took a second, but she found her voice and answered, "Yes."

"Good. I'd kiss you so slowly, all over, every beautiful, adorable inch of you, your throat, your lips, your . . . sweet shoulders. I'd run my fingers through your hair and hold you close. I want to touch you, Charity. . . ."

Aflame with his words, Charity closed her eyes as his husky, sensuous voice seemed to caress her body. In spite of their nebulous airiness, his words had a blazing effect. Breathing heavily, she clutched the phone. Hunger uncoiled, expanding with heat to permeate her veins and bones. She writhed and groaned.

"What's that, darlin? Did you say something?"

Her eyes flew open. "Oh!"

"I thought you said something to me, Charity."

Silence. She couldn't say a word. She shook and knotted the sheet in her fist. He chuckled softly. "Darlin', the song's almost over. We'll be back on the air. Call me again. Can you stay awake until the last of the show?"

She almost laughed at the ridiculousness of his question. "Yes."

"Call me during the last thirty minutes of the show, darlin'."

"I will."

And she did. She clutched the phone, burned with embarrassment, but bravely requested "Touch Me in the Morning."

" 'Touch Me in the Morning,' " he repeated, and she dissolved into jelly.

The words made her want to touch him . . . and the only man she could think of was Oregon Brown! She clenched her hands and fought to mentally see Tom Selleck instead.

"So here we are in the early hours of the mornin' and we have a request for 'Touch Me in the Morning,' " Rory said. "Beautiful. It's late. Lay your head on the pillow, darlin', close your eyes, and think of me."

The music commenced. Charity's heart pranced like a racehorse at the starting gate. The voice she waited to hear came on, speaking softly to her alone.

"Darlin', I like your request. I really like that title." His voice deepened to a purring rumble. "Darlin', are you in bed?"

She couldn't answer this time. She listened in silence to the song.

"Charity, are you there?"

"Hmmmm."

He chuckled. "What's the matter, darlin'?"

"Hmmmm."

He sighed, a tremulous breath that rasped through the line into her nervous system. How could a soft, tiny noise trigger destruction?

"Ahh, Charity, you must be sleepy, darlin'. Drowsy. I wish I could hold your sweet body next to mine."

How did he get away with indiscriminately saying things like that to women he didn't know? How did he know whether his listeners had a boyfriend or an irate husband who might walk in on the conversation? Charity wondered about it fleetingly, then tossed her curiosity aside. Who cared? She loved every word! She would miss Enid when she had to go home to Tulsa.

"Charity . . ."

She opened her eyes. Surely her mouth, throat, windpipe, and brain could function enough to get out one word. "Yes?"

"I'm so glad you called me. I can just picture you in my arms, darlin'. I want to hold you, love. Hold you and kiss you until you melt."

She did melt, into a puddle of volatile desire that hovered on the brink of spontaneous combustion.

"It's late, darlin'. I'm going to sign off soon, go home to bed."

She shook. No one had ever crammed so much sexy feeling into a one-syllable word. *B-e-d.* Only, said by Rory Runyon, it was a two-syllable word. Oh, my. Maybe she shouldn't listen to him for a few nights.

"Darlin', I have to sign off. Think about me, Charity. I'll think about you, about 'Touch Me in the Morning.' 'Night, darlin'."

"Hmmmm."

She hung up the phone, but she couldn't hang up herself. Her nerves had spun into tangled string. Knotted was more like it. She stared into the darkness, miserable, aching, and more lonely than ever. After enough flounces to twist the sheet into a rope, she sat up, turned on the bedside lamp, and looked for something to read. There was a book on the bottom shelf of the small chest beside the bed.

History of Railways in Mexico. Maybe Mexican railroads would be an antidote for Rory Runyon. She opened the book and began to read. Her eyes followed each line obediently, but her brain and her body were over a thousand miles north of Mexican railways.

A light rap on the door made her raise her head.

five

Surprised, her thoughts on other things, she answered without hesitation. "Come in."

Oregon did. He paused in the doorway, big and sexy in his tight jeans, his lashes drooping over his eyes. In his hands he held two mugs. He kicked the door shut and walked toward her. "I saw your light and thought we'd have a nightcap."

Her brain finally began to function, to stir out of the euphoria caused by Rory. Little bells began to tinkle a warning, then, as Oregon approached the bed, they started to toll like the bells of Notre Dame.

"Oregon, it's a little late." Oh, lord, she sounded so breathless!

"I know. That's why I thought you'd enjoy a nightcap." He sat down beside her and held out a mug.

She expected hot chocolate, or maybe plain milk,

but instead there was a bubbly, pale yellow liquid in the mug. "What's this?"

"Champagne. Here's to a bolt of lightning." He held out his mug.

She tried to gather her wits, along with her caution and reserve. "Listen, I can't—"

He placed his finger on her lips. "Shh. Raise your mug, Charity." He smiled. His green-gold eyes looked as inviting as a spring meadow filled with buttercups. One of his knees was pressing lightly against her thigh. He smelled so good, as he always did, and his invitation sounded harmless. She raised her mug and tapped his. He drank, his eyes never leaving hers, watching her over the rim of his white mug. The gaze was too intense, and looking into his eyes was like staring at the sun. She twiddled with the covers and sipped the bubbly champagne. Oregon set his mug on the bedside chest and reached down to tug off his boots.

"What're you doing?" She gazed at him in horror.

He smiled. Another charming, quiet smile. "My feet hurt. Do you mind?"

"No." But she knew there was a catch in it somewhere. He was up to no good. Just as sure as she drew breath, the man had evil intentions. Maybe not evil, just . . . wicked. Why was he sitting beside her at almost three in the morning, taking off his boots after being out all evening? There were a few answers, and she didn't like any of them. Maybe he had been turned down and wanted to ease his frustration. Well, that had to be straightened out quickly. "Did you just take your date home?"

His eyes began to twinkle. "No. I work at night."

"Oh! You work?"

He grinned. "Thought I was a lazy, good-for-nothing, didn't you?"

"Well, when you find a man in a hammock in the middle of the morning . . ."

". . . you ought to stretch out with him."

She laughed. She'd walked right into that one. So he had been at work. "Where do you work?" She didn't feel inclined to mention the paper, and evidently he didn't either.

"At KKZF. I go down at night, when it's quieter. I can take care of necessary business. I don't go every night." He picked up the book she'd been reading. "You're interested in railroads too? Isn't that a remarkable coincidence!"

He sounded so happy that she had to admit the truth. "No, I found it beside the bed. I couldn't sleep."

"Oh, yeah, your sleep problem. You need to relax, Charity. That's why I brought the champagne." His voice was a low rumble. While he talked, he unfastened the second button of his shirt, revealing the red-gold curls that gave his body a golden glow.

"What're you doing? Don't tell me your chest hurts!"

He smiled, a lazy smile, coaxing her to relax. "I'm hot."

She was too. She drank faster. If she finished off the champagne, he would go.

His big fingers undid another button. She stared as if drawn by a magnet. The curls covered a magnificent expanse of muscles and burnished skin. His voice lowered a fraction, reminding her of Rory Runyon's. "What did you do tonight?"

She blushed. She bent her head and wished she had long hair that would tumble forward and hide her face. He lifted her chin with his fingers. "Charity, you're blushing!" He looked both amused and satisfied. "What have you been up to?" He laughed softly. "Maybe I shouldn't ask."

"I've been listening to the radio!" she snapped, and flounced down onto the pillow, thereby committing two tactical mistakes at once.

He leaned over, placing his arms on either side of her, to pin her down. "You've been listening to 'Nighttime.' " It was a statement, not a question. It didn't matter, she couldn't have answered anyway. Oregon was so close, his marvelous mouth only a foot above her, his sweet scent teasing her, his green eyes promising excitement, his muscled arms so inviting. The golden froth of hair on his broad chest made her want to reach up and touch him. He trailed his fingers along her shoulder, as lightly as a wind song. The whispering stroke worked its own magic chemistry, changing his touch to shimmering tingles that twisted and spun through her veins.

His head lowered, his mouth met hers.

She turned her head. "Oregon, don't, please. I barely know you . . ."

"But there's a special chemistry between us," he whispered, and placed his lips firmly on hers, opening hers with an expertise that allowed no resistance. She closed her eyes and her head started spinning. One mug of champagne, Oregon's kiss, Rory's voice, and she was duck soup. In fairness she acknowledged that it was a big mug, Runyon's voice had had her quivering with readiness, and Oregon's kiss was definitely spectacular!

She squeezed her eyes shut tightly until she was whirling amid flaming reds, blues, greens, flecked with gold. Their champagne breaths mingled as their tongues danced to a silent melody.

Oregon's big hand trailed over her shoulder and down, bulldozing the polka-dot cotton out of his way. His touch was like warm sunshine as he laid his hand over her breast. Streams of sweet agony pulsed from the peak that firmed against his palm. Charity shifted, and the movement was startlingly erotic. She moaned, but his mouth caught the sound and drowned it.

Somewhere in her there should be a protest, but she couldn't locate it. She hadn't had that much champagne, but she'd been too lonely, too aroused. Her body was clamoring for more of Oregon—and he was marvelous! His kiss continued relentlessly, a sweet, throbbing agony that made her shift closer to him. She wanted him. As judgment went down, her arms went up. The fingers of one hand slipped into his luxuriant red-gold curls while her other hand trailed over his powerful shoulders.

"Touch me, Charity . . ."

Her eyes flew open. He sounded like Rory. Suddenly she wondered if he had listened to Rory's program. He would've heard Rory say her name, heard her requests. She twisted her head. "Did you listen to 'Nighttime'?"

His thick golden-brown lashes lifted slowly and his green eyes seemed to envelop her. "Sure. I heard your request, 'Touch Me . . .' And I will."

He knew! But her anger was banked before it flared into existence. His mouth returned to possess hers, to gather her moist warmth, her thoughts, her reason, and her objections, dissolving all.

Her fingers explored his solid muscles, sliding down his smooth back to his narrow waist. He felt so good to her, so right against her. Her thoughts swirled and ran together like spilled wine. Where was her long, firm resolve not to get involved with a man until she knew him well? Was she vulnerable because of loneliness or did she want Oregon that badly? Logical answers were impossible; her questions were tossed away in a tempest caused by his strong hands.

His lips trailed over her cheek, down her throat, leaving fire dancing on her skin. Oregon was slow, deliberate, so careful. His touch was gentle, arousing her with the faintest strokes, making her writhe in his arms and cling to his narrow waist. He stroked her breasts, his breath drifting over the eager nipples. She craved more until finally his tongue flicked a rosy peak. She moaned softly, twisting to thrust her hips against his hard body.

His hands were everywhere, touching her with long, slow strokes, with short, deft brushes. She wound her fingers in his hair, letting the thick, soft curls tickle her palms until he pulled away to shed his clothes. Through lowered lashes she looked at a body that was a work of art. Amber flesh dusted with freckles, broad shoulders, the narrow hips and flat, hard stomach . . . all were poetry, a song of male virility. Her gaze drifted down, and a blush seared her. He was so totally male, so big and gorgeous! He lowered himself beside her and slipped the nightie with its elasticized top down over her hips and legs, his lips following its course.

Her eyes closed as she clung to him, and she gasped as his tongue tasted her sweet flesh. No man had ever made love to her like this. Never had her body become an object of joy, of wonder. Plundering kisses drove her to abandon. She relinquished logic and cared only about Oregon. Each kiss, each stroke by his big fingers broke a link in the chain of her resistance. With his hands exploring her body, his mouth raining hot, devastating kisses, his husky voice whispering tantalizing words, he drove her to a quivering, gasping brink. His big hands molded her soft curves, heightening her need into a frenzy, until finally he parted her thighs and carefully lowered himself to her.

She clung to him wildly, arching her hips with desperate urgency. The first thrust caused a sharp stab of pain as his hard body invaded her softness, tearing into her. Her eyes flew open as she tried not to cry out.

His own eyes opened wide in shock. She realized that her status had never occurred to him. He started to withdraw, but she tightened her arms and her knees.

"Oregon," she whispered. Her hips twisted and he was beyond the point of return.

He moved slowly, carefully, his lips raining kisses on her shoulder, her throat, her mouth. Pain slowly changed, easing, transforming into sheer pleasure. When the shuddering climax came, she cried out softly while she clung to him, both frightened and exhilarated by the intense sensations. He caught her cry with his mouth, kissing her deeply as he continued to move, until he stiffened and moaned deep in his throat. She held on to him tightly as his body relaxed and lay heavily on her.

She felt complete with Oregon, floating on a silky sea of bliss. He shifted beside her, pulling her to him, fitting her head onto his shoulder, her leg over his, her soft breasts against his chest and side. He kissed her forehead and stroked her cheek, and when he spoke his voice was husky yet gentle, like spring mist.

"Ahh, Charity, darlin'."

Charity's eyes opened wide. She looked up at his firm, freckled jaw, golden lashes on a freckled cheek. No one else could say "Charity, darlin'," that same way. Oregon Brown was Rory Runyon!

Six

His lips trailed over her cheek, her temple, down to nibble her earlobe, then lower to her shoulder. "Charity, darlin', I didn't know. Why didn't you tell me?"

She barely heard the question, gave it no conscious consideration as she mulled over her discovery. Oregon Brown was Rory Runyon! Her thoughts were as busy with the revelation as ants that had discovered a lump of sugar.

Oregon propped himself up on an elbow and looked at her solemnly, brushing her tangled curls away from her face. As she gazed back at his thoughtful green eyes, his furrowed brow, she thought about Rory's deep, golden voice.

"Why didn't you tell me?" Oregon asked. "I thought . . ."

It was him, all right. Why hadn't she realized sooner? There was a difference in resonance, proba-

bly because of the microphone. Why hadn't he told
her?

"Darlin', Did I hurt you badly?"

He had known all along. All the calls, the questions. *Want to know how I'd love a woman?* Like a
boulder toppling off a cliff, her thoughts came roar-
ing down, furiously gaining momentum.

"Oh, darlin'. If you'd only told me. Charity, I
don't know what to say. . . ."

He had set her up with his sensuous voice, he had
made love to her over the phone and over the radio!
Oregon and Rory! She felt dazed. Rory Runyon
didn't tell all his callers how he'd like to make love
to them! He had told her to drive her to a quivering,
melting readiness!

"Oh, love, you're so quiet. Charity, say something
to me. This is the first time this has happened to me.
Please say something."

Well, it sure as hell was the first time it had happened to her! After all her years of caution, she had
succumbed swiftly to a husky voice and seductive
kisses! Rory Runyon, Oregon Brown! And even now
he hadn't admitted the truth. All he had done was
say, "Yes, I listened to 'Nighttime.' "

"Oh, Charity, you don't know what you're doing
to me, darlin'." He lay back down and fitted her to
his side, putting his arms around her while he gazed
up at the ceiling. She lay against him, her head on his
shoulder, her stomach pressing his hard hipbone,
their legs touching, while her thoughts churned
madly. She had been seduced by Rory Runyon! A
tingle of sheer delight danced in her veins. And it
had been so good—as good as his voice had hinted
it would be!

"Darlin', it was good. . . ."

She blinked, finally settling her attention on Oregon. She recalled the words that had drifted through a nebulous layer of consciousness in the past few minutes. *Why didn't you tell me? ... I don't know what to say.... it was good ... if you'd only told me ...*

If she had told him she was a virgin, would he have not seduced her? What was Oregon hinting at, regret? And still he didn't say, "Darlin', I have a confession. I'm Rory."

Her mind gnawed over the facts, grinding down one after another. And another whisper returned to haunt her. With the first kiss, Oregon had said, "There's a special chemistry between us." Was it special to him? She wasn't sure what she felt for Oregon, and she wanted to be very sure before she let herself get tangled up with a man.

"Charity, I wish you'd say something! Don't be angry, darlin'."

Angry? She was on a roller coaster between anger and ecstasy. She had been loved, kissed, and caressed by Rory Runyon, by Oregon Brown. Ecstasy, joy, rapture. Then down she went, with the aggravating knowledge that he had tricked her and still hadn't admitted the truth.

She mulled it over. She wouldn't tell Oregon that she knew he was Rory. She would wait and see when the truth crossed his lips. His lips. She sighed in contentment.

"Oh, Charity . . ." He shifted and gazed down at her, his thick brows drawn together, his forehead creased in a frown. Solemnly she looked up at him.

"Darlin', it was wonderful. Say something. Don't be angry over something so good."

She reached up and twisted a soft red-gold curl

around her finger. She wanted to hold him, to say she knew; she wanted to cry out, "Why didn't you tell me the truth?"

Finally she said, "It was good, Oregon."

His gaze bore into her as if attempting to discern her soul. His big hand lightly stroked her shoulder as if he needed to reassure himself she was still in his arms.

"Do you hurt?"

She shook her head, and he smiled. Joy burst inside her at the expression on his face. He looked so delighted in her, so happy! And she felt the same toward him—except, why hadn't he told her the truth? *Men.* But then, how could she expect to understand a man who kept a goat for a lawn mower?

He leaned down and kissed her ear, his moist tongue touching lightly as he whispered, "Next time, darlin', it'll be better."

Next time. The words started a blaze. Next time and next time and next time. Was she falling in love with Oregon/Rory? He settled down beside her and pulled her closer, a blissful sigh escaping his lips. " 'Night, Charity."

" 'Night, Oregon." She closed her eyes, shoving all the dilemmas into a compartment of her brain and closing it down for the night. Tomorrow she would worry about Oregon/Rory, about Aunt Mattie, about Ziza's visit and the man she wanted Charity to meet, about money and the thousand other little details that required her attention. Right now she wanted to relish Oregon's big, strong arms around her, his good, male scent, listen to his heart beat beneath her bare flesh and remember the past hour. *Charity, darlin'* . . . oooh! The mere thought made her heart jump. She had been loved by Rory

Runyon! Ecstasy! Vaguely she wondered why she had been so controlled with men in her life before, men she had dated for months and resisted without heartbreak, and then had melted for Oregon like whipped cream on burning charcoals.

Yet how could she resist? There was a spark with Oregon. Maybe too much of one sometimes, but a definite spark. His kisses were fantastic! And he was Rory Runyon. Perfection. Oregon's big body, his good-natured humor, his easygoing manner, and Rory's voice. Her sigh of contentment was a whisper in the dark. Tomorrow she would look at the problems and worry about rushing into involvement with Oregon.

Drifting on a cloud in a cotton-wrapped world of gray, Charity's first conscious awareness was of a whispered caress, a touch on her thigh. She stirred slightly, too sleep-filled to wake fully and open her eyes. The enticing tingle continued. Light, feathery touches brushed over breast and hip, across her flat stomach. She moved her hips and stretched, content, dreaming of Oregon now. Warm breath wafted over her throat, her ear. A moist tongue-tip touched her ear, and her eyes finally opened.

The room was dim, silent, and dusky with the first faint streaks of dawn. She was lying in Oregon's arms, facing him, pressed to his broad chest while he stroked and kissed her awake.

" 'Morning, darlin'," he murmured, and her temperature rose. She forgot what he had just said. Suddenly it was imperative to hold him, to touch him. She wanted his warmth, his big solid body, his magic words. She wound her arms around his neck and smiled.

" 'Morning, Oregon."

A fire blazed in his green eyes, erasing the rest of the world. "This time will be better, darlin'," he whispered before he kissed her.

Better? Better than ecstasy? The magic sparks that his kiss set off ignited her entire body, and for the next hour it never occurred to her to protest. Oregon kissed her fervently while his caresses set her aflame with longing. His big hands roamed down the sweet curve of her spine, molding her to him while his lips at her throat and ear and nape built intense desire. He shifted to kiss her breasts, the soft, full contours and the rosy, wanton peaks. He was more leisurely this time as he explored her body, discovering what aroused her until finally he possessed her completely.

He thrust into her softness, driving her to an urgency, a turbulent craving that she hadn't known was possible. She clung to him with abandon as they reached the brink, then crashed over, drifting down in a golden world of rapture.

While his weight pressed her into the bed, Oregon murmured endearments in his husky, amber voice, words that made her feel as if she belonged in his arms forever.

He rolled onto his back, pulling her to him, and together they watched the sun's glowing rays spill silently into the room, splashing across the bed, lending a rosy hue to their replete bodies.

But finally she had to face reality, had to step out of the fantastic dreamworld Oregon had created. She sat up. "Oregon, I have to get breakfast and take Aunt Mattie home."

"Lie down, darlin'. I'll cook breakfast and then take Mattie home."

"I can't stay up here in your bed! Aunt Mattie would go into shock."

He chuckled as he pulled her back down. "No, she wouldn't. I won't be here with you—not while I cook and take her home."

She pushed away from him and slid off the bed. "I can't stay in bed all day!"

He put his hands behind his head as his eyes devoured her naked body languorously. His relentless gaze sparked her modesty. Blushing, she snatched up the black satin sheet and wrapped it around her.

"Stop that, Oregon! And cover yourself, please!"

"Don't be a spoilsport, Charity. Black satin is pretty sexy on you."

"Oregon, stop! These sheets are scandalous!" And his marvelous reddish-gold body was overpowering as it lay stretched out on one.

He raised a brow. "Want to make them more scandalous?"

"No! You're oversexed!"

He shook his head, grinning crookedly, as he stood up. "No, I'm entranced, beguiled, by a gorgeous, luscious pair of . . . blue eyes."

"Oregon Brown! Stop this minute!" She thought she was going to melt, just like the Wicked Witch of the West. With a mighty effort she summoned her wits and her sternest voice, and said, "I can't lie around all day in a bed or a hammock. I have things to do."

"Oh, my, aren't we fierce this morning!" He started around the bed to her, and her heart began pounding wildly.

"Oregon . . ."

He wrapped his arms around her. "Mmmm, you smell so nice. Sweet Charity."

"I have to get dressed and go home." She sounded as firm as water. He smiled, and it took the wind out of her sails. She raised her chin and hoped that he wouldn't notice her resolve was fading. "Oregon."

"Okay, darlin'. I'm gone."

He picked up his clothes and left, leaving her in a daze. What had happened to her life? It had changed so swiftly. She couldn't imagine a time when she hadn't known Oregon. Her flesh still felt the lingering brush of his fingers. The bed was rumpled from his weight, from his marvelous big body. The sheet wrapped around her had a faint trace of his clean masculine scent. And at the moment it was impossible to summon regret for her actions.

After she had bathed and dressed, she made the bed, looking for the last time at the black satin sheets and seeing Oregon's golden body stretched out on them. Had he planned the seduction when he had made the bed up with black sheets? Was that a habit he had? She ground her teeth as she went downstairs to have breakfast with Oregon and Aunt Mattie.

Oregon, looking so appealing in his faded jeans and pale blue knit shirt, had eggs, toast, bacon, and hot coffee ready. As she watched him move around the kitchen, a thousand questions ran through her mind. She felt befuddled, as if she were caught by a force she couldn't battle, a surging sea that whirled her along on giddy currents. Every look he gave her seemed to hold its own special meaning, a confirmation of something unique and wonderful they had discovered in each other. And he couldn't stop smiling at her, showing off his dimples and making her smile right back at him, until she wondered why Aunt Mattie didn't notice the charged atmosphere.

After breakfast Charity drove downtown to talk to Mr. Wurley, the editor of the newspaper. An hour later, when she stepped outside, the hot May sunshine poured over her, shimmering on the sidewalk, making it sparkle. Across the street the courthouse on the square was shaded by tall trees. On the blocks surrounding it, people strolled in and out of shops and offices. She turned, her gaze resting briefly on the glass front of the newspaper office. She knew nothing about journalism and she had a buyer. Both she and Mr. Wurley agreed, the best thing to do would be to sell the paper to Oregon. She suspected Mr. Wurley was relieved about the decision, he knew and liked Oregon. She headed for the car to phone her attorney about her decision. An audit had already commenced, and she would need an appraisal. The paper was solvent, and from what Mr. Oppenheim, her attorney, had said, there would be enough money to set up a nice trust for Aunt Mattie.

As Charity drove home she mulled over the future. She was going to sell the paper. Now, what would she do about Aunt Mattie? The money from the sale would take care of her financially, but Mattie was too elderly to live alone, too forgetful. Charity debated giving up her own apartment and moving to Enid, or taking Aunt Mattie to Tulsa. Neither was a good idea. And even as she worried over her problems, beneath the surface of her thoughts floated an uncertain element that could affect the solutions— Oregon. Did she want to settle in Enid, find a job here, and stay close to Oregon? Would he really want her to, or had their intimacy been something casual to him? She was appalled at how little she knew about him. Yet, in ways, she felt as if she knew Oregon better than anyone else—a knowledge with a depth of quality that had nothing to do with time. Why hadn't he told her he was Rory? She remembered his laugh, his kisses, his passionate lovemaking, and a blush heated her cheeks.

Setting her jaw in a determined line, she turned around and drove back to Aunt Mattie's bank. She asked to see Mr. Simpson, the banker who had handled Uncle Hubert's affairs for years. Less than half an hour later, Charity headed home again, in more of a dilemma than ever. Mr. Simpson had politely discussed her financial situation and, to Charity's surprise, agreed to make her a loan to set her up in the landscape business in Enid if she wanted. What should she do? Stay in Enid near Mattie and Oregon and go deeper into debt, or go back to Tulsa and get a job? No easy answer had come by the time she drove up the driveway, and her thoughts had settled on Oregon. She didn't want to be like Ziza. In the past she had so carefully avoided casual relationships, then had fallen for Oregon like an uprooted tree! Well, it still wasn't too late to get to know him much better. And with that pleasant prospect in mind, she spent the rest of the afternoon helping Aunt Mattie sort through things in the garage. She was delighted when Oregon dropped by at around three, although she paid more attention to his splendid body as he moved heavy boxes and furniture for them than to her own sorting.

At five o'clock Charity asked him to stay for dinner, but he declined, saying he had to go to the station. As they stood alone in the garage, he rested his arms on her shoulders, toying with the neck of her T-shirt, stroking her throat with his fingers. She looked up into his eyes and her pulse jumped. She saw the message in those eyes, the smoldering hunger. His compelling voice was soft as he said, "I want to have you for dinner tomorrow night."

Was she in love with him—or was it merely sex? Last night had been spectacular enough to addle the most jaded mind. In her innocence, how was she to judge her emotions? She continued to stare at him, and was surprised when his brows drew together. He leaned forward and peered at her intently.

"We can just eat peanut butter sandwiches at my house if it would make it easier." He continued to study her closely. "Charity, what's on your mind?" His voice had changed suddenly, deepened, and she wondered what he had discovered in her eyes.

For just two seconds she considered blurting out the truth, that she might be in love with him. Then she remembered his deceit, his unscrupulous—was it really unscrupulous?—seduction over the airwaves with his golden, sexy voice. As she stood in indecision, one of Oregon's brows arched over his eye, giving him a devilish look. "Charity, it's just a neighborly dinner. I've already asked Mattie and she accepted for both of you."

"Why didn't you tell me!" she exclaimed angrily.

"I wanted to see what you'd say."

"You know, you have a deceitful streak in you!"

He blushed! A red flush crept up his cheeks, suffusing his face with a rosy glow. It served him right.

"My intentions are good," he said, so sincerely that she felt mollified. If he had stopped there, he would have been ahead, but he added, "Even if my actions aren't."

The teasing gleam was back in his eyes. She didn't know what she felt and she didn't have the smallest inkling about Oregon's feelings, so she kept quiet and didn't say a word.

"I've got to run, honey," he said. The look in his green eyes was inviting, and she leaned toward him a fraction of an inch. His arms went around her instantly and he kissed her. Soundly. So soundly she forgot where she was, that Aunt Mattie might walk in on them, that she didn't want to rush into an affair, that Oregon could be aggravating. She loved every second of his kiss and returned it with enthusiasm. Finally he released her slightly, raising his head to gaze into her eyes. "You have the bluest eyes I've ever seen, Charity. So big and blue I feel I could drown in them."

Each word was a drop of hot, sweet syrup running through her insides. She trembled, and her hands tightened on his hard biceps. "For someone who spends his days lying in a hammock, you have some big muscles."

He smiled, a slow lifting of the corners of his perfect mouth. "I do a few other things." He could make anything sound suggestive. Sound deliciously naughty and enticing. She wanted to wrap her arms around him and cling forever. His arms tightened a fraction. "I'm going to be late for an appointment. I have a meeting at my office in fifteen minutes."

"I'm not keeping you," she said, but her mind wasn't on what she was saying. It was concentrating on green eyes, a beautiful mouth, a strong body . . .

He leaned down for one more long kiss that left her dazed when he released her. He touched the tip of her nose with his forefinger. " 'Bye, hon. I'll miss you tonight. See you tomorrow."

" 'Bye, Oregon," she whispered. She watched him stride down the driveway, his broad shoulders swinging a fraction, golden curls ruffled by the wind, his long legs covering the distance easily, his tight jeans clinging to narrow hips and trim buttocks. And she remembered in the finest detail every inch of his golden skin. "Oh, my," she breathed softly. "Oregon Brown."

She wandered into her room, closing the door for privacy, and stared at her image in the dresser mirror. She looked as if she had been kissed. Or struck by lightning. Her lips were slightly red, swollen from Oregon's touch. She tried to raise one eyebrow the way he did. Both brows climbed. She couldn't do it. She held one brow and tried to raise the other. How did he manage that look? With both brows arched she looked in shock; he had looked so sexy. Her toes curled as she stared into the mirror and saw Oregon, one brow raised, his gaze intent and mocking, teasing her.

And then it dawned on her that if they went to dinner, he would have to tell her about Rory Runyon because he would have to go to work. Except Aunt Mattie would be with her and they would go home early. Well, she'd fix that! As she turned away to go back to work, a smile curved her rosy lips.

When the evening came, Charity felt an inner tension coiling and tightening. She couldn't wait to hear "Nighttime"! Would Oregon reveal his identity? Her nerves were raw with anticipation. She told Aunt Mattie good night, worked furiously cleaning out kitchen drawers, then bathed, taking her time, scrubbing herself, reliving every glorious second of the previous night. She dressed in a pale blue cotton nightie, then looked over the list of titles she wanted to request on "Nighttime." She would give Oregon pause for thought! What did she feel for him? Was she dazzled by a seduction that had occurred by default, simply because she was so lonely? Or was it deeper than that? She switched off the lights, climbed into bed, and turned on the radio. The red light from the dial glowed over the sheets as the familiar theme song filled the darkened bedroom. And then Rory Runyon was on.

Seven

"Welcome to 'Nighttime.' This is station KKZF, coming to you for the next two hours with your favorites, with music for the magic of midnight, soft mood music to lull you to sleep, to play in the background, to bring back memories." He spoke in mellow, drowsy tones that stroked her senses like strong, deft fingers.

Charity sighed and slithered down under the sheet. How could she not have known it was Oregon? Of course Rory and Oregon were the same. There was that marvelous voice that made Oregon's chest rumble slightly when he talked. The voice that was like melted butter oozing over every sensitive, quivering nerve. Rory Runyon had held her in his arms last night, kissed her! and made love to her! Charity blushed and tingled and ached and worried. Was she rushing into a relationship as swiftly as Ziza did? And as disastrously? She shuddered at the memory of that year she had spent with Ziza, then shoved the memory aside, exchanging it for thoughts of Oregon.

"We'll start off tonight, darlin'," he was saying in his sexy voice, "with one just 'specially for you. This is to you. Here's 'Would You Be My Lady?' "

As the country music began, she wondered if he had chosen the song to send her a message in the title. Her heart thudded against her ribs.

As she listened to the song, her thoughts buzzed like busy little bees. Why hadn't Oregon told her he was Rory Runyon? Maybe he would tomorrow night. But she would teach him a lesson tonight! He had set her up last night, come home to a quivering mass of frustrated woman, and seduced her. And the memory turned her to jelly again.

The music ended. "There, darlin', did you like that? I hope so. Isn't this a marvelous night? Another nice evening like last night." His voice thickened, becoming so warm, so seductive. "Wasn't last night the best ever?" Charity sighed blissfully as he continued, "Tonight the temperature's seventy degrees, with a breeze and a full moon. Have you seen that moon? It's a big white pearl in the black sky. I'd like to sit in the moonlight and hold you in my arms. Would you like that, darlin'? Just sit and listen to the next song. How's this? 'You Oughta Be Home with Me'? Let's listen."

Soft music and Barry Manilow's voice drifted into the darkened room, and Charity bit her lip. Was Oregon/Rory playing these songs to tell her something? Or was she imagining that they might be for her? She listened to Oregon's chatter in between songs, and to two more records, "My One and

Only" and "Waiting for You." Then he asked for requests.

She sat up, dialed frantically, and listened to the phone ring. His voice came over the radio and the phone. "Hi, there. This is Rory Runyon of 'Nighttime,' at station KKZF."

"Rory, this is Charity."

"Charity."

She slipped beneath the sheet and tried to catch her breath.

"Darlin', I'd hoped you'd call. What song would you like to hear?"

Sweet revenge. " 'The Men in My Life.' "

He coughed. " 'The Men in My Life'? That's an unusual request, but I'll play it for you. Don't go away, darlin'. Here's your request." The song began, and Oregon's throaty voice came over the wire. "Charity, you've been holding out on me. The men in your life—I thought I might be the *man* in your life."

She looked at the phone. Now, why couldn't he have said that to her last night when he held her close? Men were impossible to understand! "You are, Rory," she answered breathlessly, so full of sincerity she was struck by wonder at herself.

"I belong to a group?"

"No, it's just you."

"Then you should've requested 'The Man I Love,' or some song like that."

"Well, there's another man . . . but you're the one I really want to know."

"You're just saying that because it's safe."

"No, Rory, I'm not."

"Another man." He said it like a death knell. Like the voice of doom.

"I'd trade him for you." Now she was marching straight into deep water. Revenge? She might drown in the waters she stirred up.

"Darlin', I'm overcome! I'm just a voice in the night."

"Oh, but you're so sensitive, so . . . much more honest with me."

He coughed again. "Charity, I . . ."

She waited. And waited. The long red second hand on her clock swept on steadily. "Yes?" she finally said.

"Maybe you're judging him too harshly. Tell me about this other man in your life, darlin'."

Now *he* was treading on dangerous ground! "Well, Rory, I've met someone and I like the way he kisses."

There was a flurry of coughs. "Oh, darlin', you do?"

"Yes, but he still doesn't have what you do. Your sensitivity. I can talk to you. You talk to me. That's important. More important than spectacular kisses, don't you think?"

His voice was in the basement, down so low, it practically sent vibrations over the phone wires. "Damn, we're at the end of the song. Call me back, dar—"

As the music faded Charity grinned and wriggled her toes. Chalk one up for her, Mr. Oregon Brown. Put that in your noggin and think about it! It was the first time she had ever heard Oregon swear. Usually it was "Mercy" or "My!" or some other mild word. She smoothed the sheet as his voice came from the radio.

"There we have it, 'The Men in My Life.' Charity, darlin', you call in again, will you?"

"Sure, Rory."

"That's good. I'll be waiting. Don't forget me. Now, we'll take a little break here to talk about something scrumptious, Henrietta's Apple Pie Mix. Yu-um-yum."

Oregon's drawling "yum-yums" sent Charity's pulse into flight. In husky tones that sounded as seductive as his usual patter, he urged his listeners to try Henrietta's Pie Mix. "You want something that will melt in your mouth? That is so delicious you'll have to come back for more?" Charity wriggled. Henrietta should sell a whopping big amount of pie mix. "Just reach out and pick up Henrietta's Pie Mix the next time you're in the store."

Each word made her want to reach out for Oregon! He added softly, insinuatingly, "Oh, it's so tantalizing. Your taste buds will thank you. Just try Henrietta's Pie Mix and see for yourself. Don't take my word for it. Pick some up tomorrow.

"Now, ready for some music again? Here's another oldie. I've been waiting all day to play it. Are you listening, darlin'? Good, here goes." In a languorous voice he said, " 'Upstairs in My House.' "

"Upstairs in My House"! He was playing it to her for last night! It was a rock song by Men At Work and had a lively beat that wasn't going to put anyone to sleep. It wasn't typical of the music played on 'Nighttime.' He had to have chosen it for the title! Why was he so vocal as Rory Runyon and so evasive as Oregon Brown! Maybe he had a guilty conscience about setting her up for seduction last night!

The next song was a request from someone named Dinah. Charity lay in the dark and wondered what Oregon was saying to Dinah while the song played. How many women were in his life? How seriously had he been involved with one in his past? She knew so little about him. And so much. Her lashes fluttered closed while she thought about his kisses.

The song ended, and he played two more, titles that meant nothing to her. Maybe she had imagined the others were meant to convey a message to her. Then he asked for requests again. She sat up, dialed quickly, and felt her heart jump when he said, "Hi, there."

"Rory, it's me, Charity."

"Good, darlin'. I'm so glad you called again. What would you like to hear now?"

" 'Why Do People Lie?' "

" 'Why Do People Lie?' Fine. You know, that'll wake everyone up, darlin'. That's a red-hot Kenny Loggins."

"I know. You won't play it?"

"It's coming right up now. Hang on to your seats out there. Here we go."

The heavy beat filled the room, and Charity held her breath.

"Charity. We're not on the air now. Darlin', no one should lie to you. I know just how sweet you are."

She slipped down in bed, cradling the phone between her ear and shoulder. It was hard to get her breath. "Thank you, Rory. You don't really know."

"Charity . . ."

And she knew he was on the brink of telling her again. And again he didn't.

"Yes?"

"Tell me some more about the man you like to kiss."

Her eyes flew open. Why wouldn't he admit his